STORIES FROM ERINNA

TIES

Friends and family greet Lady Ira Macaria as she alights from the coach that brought her to Oedran. With no idea why she was sent home, she must face the consequences and the King. Now, more than ever, she must marry the right man to save her family's reputation and secure their dynasty. As navigating Oedranian society and rekindling old friendships takes unexpected turns, she must confront her future and her past...

Copyright

Trigger Warning

This book is fantasy set in a pre-Victorian style civilisation. Although not explicit there may be references to unacceptable behaviours. Subjects such as child mortality and fatal illnesses are mentioned but not explored in any depth.

TIES

The Erinnan Legacy

Stories From Erinna

J.A.Cauldwell

<u>Dedication</u>
For Sybil
who wished to know more about Ira

Pennod
Press

Character lists and notes on world building
are at the end of the book

THE ERINNAN LEGACY

TREASON AND TRUTH

FROM THE PAST COMES MAGIC,
FROM THE PRESENT, DANGER,
GRADUALLY COLLIDING

TREASON
TERA
TRAPPED
TRAGEDY

STORIES FROM ERINNA

EVERYBODY HAS A STORY AND SOMEBODY KNOWS IT

Standalone stories that may link to characters from other series.

TIES

For freebies, The Court Newsletter and to see more details and information on works in progress, please visit https://erinna.co.uk.

MAPS

THE OEDRANIAN EMPIRE

OEDRAN AND ENVIRONS

1: Macarian House | 2: Landis House
3: Master Netherhind's | 4: Latimer's Bookshop
5: Rale House | 6: Ryson House
7: Palace of Oedran
8: Wynwood (North of Oedran)

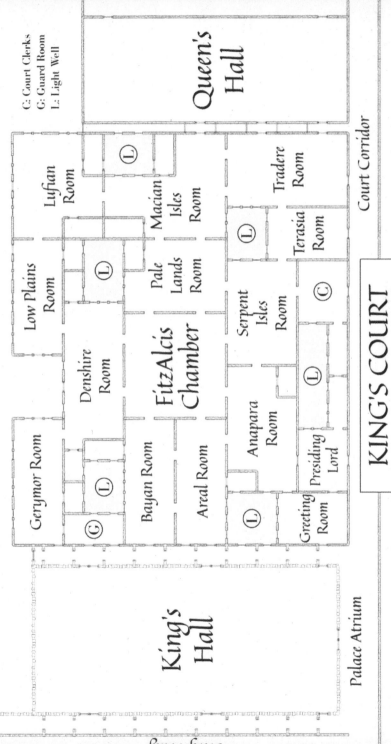

FITZALCIS FAMILY TREE

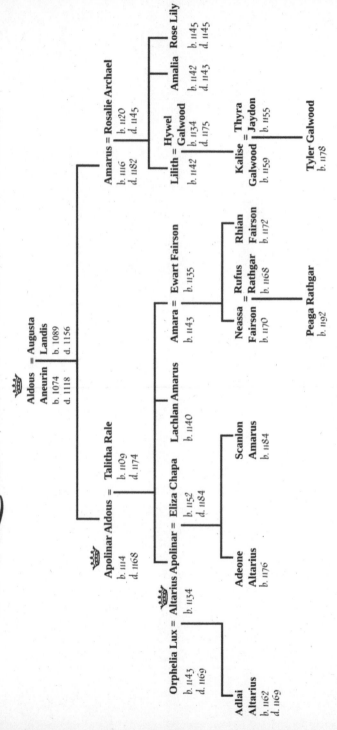

Aldous Aneurin = Augusta Landis
b. 1074, d. 1118 — b. 1089, d. 1156

Apolinar Aldous = Talitha Rale
b. 1114, d. 1168 — b. 1109, d. 1174

Altarius Apolinar = Eliza Chapa
b. 1134 — b. 1152, d. 1184

Lachlan Amarus
b. 1140

Amarus = Rosalie Archael
b. 1116, d. 1182 — b. 1120, d. 1145

Orphelia Lux = Altarius Apolinar
b. 1143, d. 1169 — b. 1134

Adlai Altarius
b. 1162, d. 1169

Adeone Altarius
b. 1176

Scanlon Amarus
b. 1184

Amara = Ewart Fairson
b. 1143 — b. 1135

Neassa Fairson = Rufus Rathgar
b. 1170 — b. 1168

Rhian Fairson
b. 1172

Peaga Rathgar
b. 1192

Hywel Galwood = Lilith
b. 1134, d. 1175 — b. 1116, d. 1182

Amalia
b. 1142, d. 1143

Rose Lily
b. 1145, d. 1145

Kalise Galwood = Thyra Jaydon
b. 1142 — b. 1159 — b. 1155

Tyler Galwood
b. 1178

LANDIS / MACARIA

FAMILY TREE

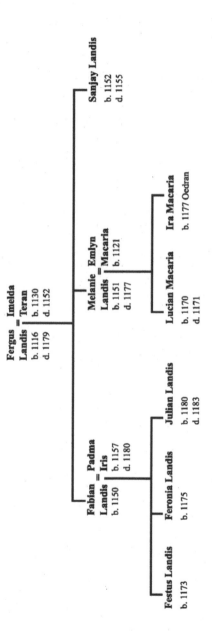

Fergus = Imelda
Landis   Teran
b. 1116 b. 1130
d. 1179 d. 1152

Fabian = Padma
Landis   Iris
b. 1150 b. 1157
         d. 1180

Festus Landis
b. 1173

Feronia Landis
b. 1175

Julian Landis
b. 1180
d. 1183

Melanie = Emlyn
Landis   Macaria
b. 1151 b. 1121
d. 1177

Lucian Macaria
b. 1170
d. 1171

Ira Macaria
b. 1177 Oedran

Sanjay Landis
b. 1152
d. 1155

TIES

Chapter 1
ARRIVING HOME

LADY IRA MACARIA alighted from the coach that had brought her home to Oedran in a thoughtful mood. Recalling the trepidation in which she'd left for Garth, she hadn't expected the same emotion to greet her return. Garth had been vibrant and exhilarating, the Citadel Court had seemed far freer than she expected and her hosts had been warm and welcoming. Her recall to Oedran had come without explanation and little notice.

She thanked the footman who helped her alight and gazed with fresh eyes at her childhood home. Its pale stone seemed far removed from the warmer tones of Garth. She caught the eye of the groom holding the coach horses.

"Lex! It's good to see you."

"Likewise, my lady. Welcome home. Aunt Maria will be pleased to see you."

"Your father's in his study, m'lady," stated the head groom ambling over. "Said to tell you to go straight there."

"Thank you, Jack. I take it you're well?"

"Well enough, m'lady. No complaints. I hope your journey was pleasant."

She nodded before leaving for the house. Had it been her imagination or had Jack interrupted her talk with Wynfeld on purpose? Well, they were no longer children running around together. She'd been sent to Garth to break the link with that childhood.

Her old nurse was loitering in the entrance hall. With a grin, Ira crossed to her. Maturity would wait. The hug lasted a long moment and was full of a year's absence.

"Look at you, my lady. All grown and elegant."

Ira chuckled and twirled. "Do you like it? Lady Galwood helped me choose the material."

"Always did say strong colours suited you. Now, get you to His Lordship. He's been fretting since dawn, expecting you'd have trouble on the road."

"I doubt he ever frets like that." She ran lightly up the stairs to her father's study. Catching her breath, she rearranged her dress. The blue silk still made her smile.

Knocking, she entered the study after waiting for the reply. Her father might be indulgent occasionally, but he was no less strict for that. She crossed to stand in front of his desk to her right. The light behind him made his face dark and brooding.

"Ah. You're here. Good."

'Fretting indeed,' thought Ira. That was not her father. Straight, to the point, direct, a military man through and through. Not someone who fretted. Let alone over her.

"Yes, father. I'm here. How are you?"

"Hmm. Immaterial. Her Elegance wrote."

Her mind racing, Ira said, "Princess Lilith was very kind to me, father."

"She thought you'd be better here. Why?"

"I don't know, sir." Was she in trouble? She wracked her brains, trying to recall anything she'd done to outrage the Princess. There wasn't anything she remembered. She certainly hadn't indulged in frivolities like some of the Garth ladies.

"Well, Her Elegance wasn't forthcoming on the reasons for sending you home. Make no mistake, Ira, she sent you home. She wrote to His Majesty as well. It has led to an interesting discussion. When you recall what you did, I want to know."

Ira swallowed. "I… Father, I have no idea. I honestly have none. I was being the epitome of decorum. I never saw anyone alone. I never danced too often with the same gentleman. I never rode alone – not even if it was with a groom. I didn't shop alone or take dancing lessons alone. In fact, some courtiers laughed at me because I wouldn't break with convention. I thought as a guest of His Excellency, it was better not to. If I had any idea, I'd tell you, father. I really would." She blinked back tears. Why had Princess Lilith sent her away? She hadn't thought she had insulted her or her son's hospitality.

Lord Macaria frowned. "Very well. We'll attend Court tomorrow. For tonight, I want you to write a letter of thanks to Lady Galwood."

Ira left the study no less perplexed than when she'd alighted from the coach and possibly more so. She walked along the landing to her room and sank onto the bed, staring at nothing. She bit at her lip. Maybe there had been something, something she'd work out in time, but until then she'd better write the letter and attend to her household duties.

* * *

As she signed off her letter of thanks to Lady Galwood, she hesitated, glancing at the parchment stack. Would it hurt to write to Princess Lilith as well? She might think it too forward and if she then informed the King, there'd likely be further disgrace, but she had thought they had found a friendship with talk of Oedran and the city. Her Elegance hadn't been home since her marriage and, although that had seemed happy, she had a somewhat strained relationship with her wed-daughter. It had been nice for them to talk of home. Mind made up, she pulled a fresh piece of parchment towards her. The Princess might never reply, but she would feel better if she had tried to lay an issue to rest. When she finished that carefully worded letter, she retrieved a third piece of parchment and wrote to Tyler Galwood. It might be unusual, but he had been gallant towards her during her stay. Never more forward than a brother would have been and rather less honest than one. Her closest male relative of her own age was her cousin Festus, and he was far too honest at times. She smiled to herself. It would be good to see him. Tomorrow, maybe? She should pay a few calls before attending Court. As she signed the letter to Tyler, she planned whom to call on. Her cousins were top of her list. Festus and Feronia would want all the stories. Cornelia Rale, possibly she'd let Finn and young Aelia join them for the stories, or some of them. Maybe she'd call and see young Leila Ryson as well whose brother Elidir wouldn't bother them. He was wrapped up with Prince Scanlon's friendship. Leila might even be at Rale House if she was lucky.

She addressed and sealed the letters, before bundling them together into another sealed pouch and addressing it to Lord Galwood. That would mean no-one else would read the contents. Or she hoped it would. Interfering with the Exarch's post was more than most people's lives were worth. She crossed the hallway between the drawing room and estate office and, knocking, entered without waiting for a reply. The steward pushed himself to his feet.

"Welcome home, my lady. It's good to see you."

"Thank you, Piers. I've some letters for Garth. Can you see they're despatched by special rider? I wouldn't like to insult Her Elegance with tardiness."

"I'll see it done, my lady. Is there anything else?"

"Well, as I'm here…"

She seated herself with the poise she'd gained in Garth. Princess Lilith's words echoed in her mind: *'A young lady never sinks onto a chair. She sits with deliberation and grace. Legs together, back straight. You are what matters. Everything else should fade into the background.'* She could almost see the steward readjust as he took in her deliberate movements. The child was gone, his face said.

Ira chuckled. "Father sent me to Garth to polish the effects of growing up without a mother, Piers."

"Her Ladyship would be proud of whom you have become."

"I hope so. How's father been?"

The steward hesitated. "He's glad you're home, my lady. Let's leave it there."

Ira bit her lip. Realising it, she hastily rearranged her features. "I'm glad to be home. Is there anything I should know about? Any changes?"

"Mary left, my lady. Married young Tom Warren but he died not long after of stupidity. Got himself kicked by a horse. Never did have much sense. She's all right, before you start fretting. His mother's taken her in. I'm hearing whispers she's marrying one of their neighbours. A good lad. Scribe up at the Courthouse. She'll do all right for herself. We've a couple of new maids as Liza married too. They've been here a few weeks. Good girls. I don't think they'll give trouble. Maria approved when she returned from visiting her brother. Your father's left a lot of the oversight in her hands since my wife died."

Ira swallowed. "I was sorry I was away then. I watched the stars for her. Was it long?"

"Not in the end. As to other news, we're much as we were when you left. Jack's keeping the stables in order. The kitchen's under the eye of Maria and Abe, and the gardens, well, Whyte will be glad to see you home. He's been saying all year, 'The young mistress needs to see this blooming...' occasionally he'd stop himself, so I think he was going to say 'blooming mess,' but I couldn't possibly have mentioned that."

Ira chuckled. "I'll have a cup of tea with him soon. I've missed the garden here. Garth's gardens were beautiful, but not the same. I never felt as relaxed in them. Always felt like I couldn't touch them. Do you know what Abe's planned for meals for the next week?"

"Not a clue, my lady. I doubt he has. Should I warn him you're asking?"

Ira shrugged. "Not today. I'm sure I'll enjoy whatever is for dinner. I'll leave you to your work."

With an odd feeling of loneliness, she re-entered the drawing room whose windows overlooked the gardens. A fireplace to her left was swept clean and laid and on her right was the sideboard. Idly she ran her fingers along its polished edge as she crossed to the windows. Had she really been away for so long? It felt like no time at all. There was something oddly disturbing about that. The gardens were full of autumn colours. She needed to see Whyte soon. Her father would start fretting about the leaf litter in the next week or so. It should be removed to compost. Turning to the room, she shivered, wondering what to do. Getting the fire lit would be a start. Had her father been so distracted he'd forgotten the house needed warming? Ringing the bell, she seated herself at the desk. She should at least seem busy. She was halfway through writing a note to her Cousin Feronia when the footman entered.

"Could you see to fires please, Leo? Here, the dining room and the bedchambers. Then I'll have letters that need delivering to Landis House if you could return for them when you've seen to the fires."

"Of course, milady. Welcome home."

"Thank you. How have you been?"

"Ah, the same, milady."

"I'm glad things haven't changed. Could you let the stables know I'll be taking an early ride, please? I'll need a groom to go with me."

"I'll let Wynfeld know, never fret."

She considered saying someone else would be fine but she'd be lying. She wanted to catch up on Lex's news. He'd not written, though he'd said he would. She supposed it would have looked a little suspicious to be getting letters from her family's groom.

When the footman was leaving, she added, "Can you ask Maria to join me, please?"

* * *

A couple of minutes later, her old nurse appeared, carrying a tray of tea and biscuits. "Abe thought we'd need these, my lady."

Ira chuckled. "I might have sent for you to ask about the household."

"After speaking with Piers? I'll not believe it and nor will anyone else. Leave the notes. I doubt they're needed. Your cousins and uncle called by yesterday to make sure His Lordship was well. They know you're due home today. If they're not expecting you in the morning, I'm not breathing. So, you've grown into your skin at last."

"Princess Lilith said my governesses had done a good job, but they couldn't add polish," revealed Ira, amused.

"Hmm. Well, Mistress Fairson was dedicated, but I expect Her Elegance brought a more refined flavour to her teaching. What's she like?"

Ira sat opposite Maria and curled her feet into her chair. "Very kind, but she knows what she likes to see. I suppose all the FitzAlcis must be like that, yet she felt like a mother without enough children. She wasn't soft on me, but she spoilt me occasionally. I like her. The Citadel Court all admire her but... I don't think they are pandering to her. She's won their respect."

"She was loved here. The city sent her off to Bayan with a pageant and a city strewn with flowers, apparently."

"She mentioned it. Along with her imprisonment during the rebellion and how well father served His Majesty during those weeks."

Maria chortled. "Aye, your father did that. The image of all the lords dressed ready for battle with shining breastplates will stay with me. I'd come to the city to find work. Your ma was kind when she heard I'd come from the Macarian lands. Took me on, no questions asked. She caught the fever, o'course. Most of us did, but I nursed her through it. She was never strong after. Lost a few childer because of it."

Ira started, almost spilling her tea.

"Didn't you know? Aye. Why would you? You mother had a son who lived less than a year and two miscarriages. She feared so much when she carried you but, in the end, she was the one who left your father. He doesn't like talking about it."

Ira swallowed. "You said father fretted..."

"He loves you, Ira. He wants to see you settled and happy."

21

Ira glanced around the room. "I'm… It's not like I'll be destitute if I don't marry in the next few years. I'm his heiress and thanks to ancient Macian law, I can inherit the lordship to go down my line."

"I know, my lady, but it's a parent's job to worry about their young. Now, talking about being settled," she crooked a knowing eyebrow. "Anyone in Garth who might be worth writing to?"

Ira chuckled. "You are a dreadful influence. There were several who tried their absolute hardest to catch my attention. One literally fell over the other in asking me to dance."

"What did you do?"

"Oh, I smiled sweetly and told them they would have to come to an accommodation as I wasn't in the mind to disoblige or favour either of them, but if they drew blood, I'd dance with neither of them."

Maria laughed. "What happened?"

"They tossed a coin. The following evening, I danced with the loser first. It seemed to keep them both sweet."

"Just danced?"

"Just danced," confirmed Ira. "I wasn't reckless at all. I promise. I did have some fun though. Princess Lilith might have helped a bit more than I realised as well. I never wanted for company. In fact, it feels quite strange to be without it here."

"So I'm not company then?" asked Maria.

"You're more than company," replied Ira, snapping a biscuit. "How's Lex been?"

"Working hard. You'll spoil your dinner."

"You brought the biscuits."

Chapter 2
RIDING HIGH

IRA AWOKE THE FOLLOWING MORNING contemplating the day ahead. She'd ride out to Wynwood. Her father wouldn't object if she took a groom with her. The sun was shining through the mists, and breakfast wouldn't be for a couple of hours.

Her maid had laid everything out. There was no need to ring for her to help: riding habits were rarely laced tightly and she could manage these stays on her own. She'd have to pick out something else for visiting and for Court later. Her heart sank. If Princess Lilith had written to the King, she would have to answer his questions and, at Court, that would be tricky as she had no notion why she'd been sent home.

She left the house feeling oddly free. The caution needed in Garth was also required in Oedran, but at least she knew the groom riding with her well, and no-one would look askance at her riding with a member of her own household. She patted her mare's neck as she looked about for Wynfeld. He strolled to join her, leading his horse. Not a Swiftfoot like hers, but no less impressive.

"Morning, my lady."

"Morning, Lex."

A cough behind her preceded, "He prefers 'Wynfeld' now, m'lady."

Ira chuckled. "Does he, Pretyman?"

Torn between amusement and frustration at being outmanoeuvred, Jack eyed her. "That's me told then. Aye, I know. Times change. Just don't make me regret letting him go with you, m'lady. Where are you off to?"

"Wynwood." She gave Jack a hug. "We'll be sensible."

He hugged her back as though she was still six and tripping him up. "You be that, m'lady. Don't want to have to carry you back."

By the time they'd manoeuvred their horses through the crowds around the King's Gate and then through the busy streets beyond, the day was bright and clear, with the early mists evaporating before their eyes. The autumnal colours were less in evidence in the city, but, once out through the Paras Gate, the congestion eased and Wynfeld drew level with her.

She smiled sideways at him. "What do you think Jack meant about us behaving ourselves?"

"I can think of a few things. As long as your dress isn't covered in mud, we've been good."

She laughed. "True. *Do* you prefer Wynfeld these days?"

He shrugged. "Doesn't matter what I prefer. It's what's normal. I'm used to it. His Lordship prefers we use our family names – well, unless it's people like Jack whom he's known for years."

"True," mused Ira. "I hear Mary was married and widowed."

"Yes. She's not had an easy time. We're keeping an eye on her until she's wed again. Maria would have taken her back, but I don't think she wanted to return."

"I wish she had though. I don't like to think of her struggling. Have you heard anything from Liza?"

"Not beyond the fact she's happy. Or she seemed to be, anyway."

"And what do you think of the new maids?" asked Ira with a grin.

"They have nothing on my lady."

"I'd hope they were wearing something," replied Ira innocently.

Wynfeld chuckled. "You're incorrigible, you really are."

She smiled sweetly. "I'm a lady."

He crooked an eyebrow. "You are indeed. Though, as far as I can tell, I'm not sure that means you have to be ladylike."

She snorted. "My manners have been polished in Garth; they should shine here."

"I'm blinded by them," muttered Wynfeld. "My lady, move over. His Highness is riding this way."

Ira moved her horse to the side of the paved road and inclined her head as Prince Adeone passed. He never noticed, but his companion did. Her Cousin Festus winked at her, but said nothing else. Obviously, he didn't want a public reunion.

Ira waited until they were out of earshot before she said, "He always makes me uncomfortable."

"Who, my lady?"

"His Highness. He just doesn't see anything unless he wants to."

Wynfeld frowned. "Isn't that what everyone does?"

"No. I mean, it's like he views the world but doesn't see anything unless there's a purpose to seeing it."

Wynfeld shrugged. "I guess he can do that, my lady. Maybe he has to see too much."

"Maybe. Come on, I'll race you."

"That wouldn't be being sensible— Oh, why do I bother," muttered Wynfeld, galloping after her.

By the time they had reached the outskirts of Wynwood, Ira was laughing as though she hadn't a care in the world. She turned in the saddle. "You're getting slow."

"You've a much better mount, my lady."

"True." She patted the mare's neck. "You're getting staid now you're an adult. Let's amble round the woodland and you can tell me everything about the household I'm not meant to know."

* * *

They arrived at Macarian House with twelve minutes to spare before breakfast. Jack eyed them, chortling to himself.

"Did you enjoy the gallop, m'lady?"

"I did, thank you." She paused. "My hair's a mess, isn't it?"

"It's certainly less ordered than it was, m'lady. It's good to see colour in your cheeks, but you might want to sort it before His Lordship sees it."

She ran up to her room and ran her brush hastily through the locks before plaiting the thick, black strands into order.

Rather flustered, she hurried to the dining room. Unheedingly, she opened the door. Someone grabbed her by the waist.

She squealed before turning and thumping Festus on the chest. "You—"

"Now, now... I thought you'd become a lady."

She fell into his hug. "And I thought you were with the Prince."

"I claimed urgent family business. Father and Nia don't know I'm here."

Ira chuckled. "I'm glad. You've got to tell me all the political Court gossip. Nia and Cornelia won't."

"Have I now? Hmm. I'm not sure there's much that would interest you. After all, a lady shouldn't be—"

"You can stop that," replied Ira. "Come on, Fes. I can't go to Court ignorant of the latest news. Which reminds me, have you found a wife?"

Festus sat at the table, grinning. "No. I have two excuses. The first, I don't have to marry yet. The second, it would be unwise of me to do so before the Prince is wed. Else it could appear that I'm abandoning him."

Ira laughed. "I doubt that."

He crooked an eyebrow. "Name the friend of a prince or king who married before they did."

Ira frowned. "That's not how it works."

"Isn't it?" replied Festus, helping himself to toast. "I think you'll find— Oh. Morning, Uncle Macaria."

"Morning, young Festus. Ira, did you go for a ride?"

"I did, father. Just to Wynwood. A groom went with me."

"Good. What plotting have I disturbed?"

"No plotting, uncle," replied Festus. "Ira was just talking about marriage."

Eyes narrowed at her innocent looking cousin, Ira added, "Yes, father, I was. His."

Her father chuckled. "He can't marry until Prince Adeone does."

"See," said Festus triumphantly. "It's well known."

Ira sighed. "So when's Prince Adeone going to ask Nia?"

Festus shrugged. "There's no saying he will. There's no understanding between them."

"They're close."

"That doesn't mean he'll marry her," said Macaria. "Princes rarely marry where they love. King Altarius will pick Prince Adeone's bride. As King Apolinar picked Lady Orphelia for him. She should never have died."

Ira hesitated. "Queen Eliza seemed nice, from what little I remember."

"She was, but that doesn't mean Queen Orphelia should have died. That fever had many consequences."

Ira smiled sadly at him. "Maria and I spoke of it last night."

"She said. It's in the past. So, young Festus, why are we graced with your presence this morning?"

Festus shrugged. "Nia can't bother me if she doesn't know where I am, uncle. I was also out riding with His Highness. I passed Ira and her escort, so thought I'd call by. I hope you don't mind."

"As long as His Highness didn't need your company, I don't. It's good to see you. How go your studies?"

* * *

An hour later, Festus and Ira rode the short distance to Landis House. Dismounting in the stableyard, Festus put his arm around Ira's shoulders.

"You know, your father doesn't trust me at all."

Ira chuckled. "I can't imagine why. Where's Nia likely to be?"

"Drawing room. Is that it? I'm dismissed?"

"Probably. At least for now. Anyway, don't you have lectures?"

"Only according to the lecturers. Fine. I'll leave you two talking dresses. I like that one, by the way."

Ira watched him go with a smile. She turned to make her way to the drawing room and beamed. "Uncle Landis. It's good to see you."

"You're looking very grown up, little Ira. How was Garth?"

"Enlightening. I'm here to see Nia. Do you mind?"

"No. Not at all. Where did Festus find you?"

"At home. We'd crossed paths on a morning ride, but he was with His Highness. So he called by home when he was free."

"Ah. Well, Nia's through there. Ring for anything you want."

Watching him amble off to his study, it struck Ira how different he was to his son, and not for the first time. Festus carried life lightly; her uncle carried it as though it was an unendurable burden.

Chapter 3
GOSSIP
Mid-morning
Landis House – Drawing Room

IRA ENTERED THE DRAWING ROOM still grinning. Landis House was a second home. Its rooms as familiar to her as those at Macarian House. She and Feronia had often played together, shared lessons and exchanged ailments. The hug of reunion lasted a long moment.

"I'm so glad you're home!" exclaimed Nia. "I've missed you so much."

"You seemed to be enjoying Cornelia's company."

"Oh, I do, I am, but it's not the same. Come and sit down. I've persuaded our cook that cake is just what we need and William has promised me he'll keep Festus out of our hair."

"He's failed," said Ira, carefully arranging her skirts. "Fes dropped by Macarian House. He passed me on our morning ride, so came for breakfast. It does mean we get the morning to ourselves though."

"Good. Though if he doesn't attend lectures soon, I'm not sure what will happen."

"They won't throw him out of the Advisors' School. It would cause too much upheaval. Especially as he's friends with Prince Adeone."

Nia pulled a face. "He uses that far too much. I don't think the lecturers believe him. Not since Faran started at the school. He's living at the Palace and still makes his lectures."

"He's not as close to the Prince. Talking of whom, has he proposed yet?"

Nia blushed scarlet. "No."

Ira laughed. "I'm sure he will. He obviously enjoys your company, from what I've been hearing."

"Father says not to get too close, but he says it to Fes as well. It's nonsense. It can't be bad to be close to the Prince. I don't think Lord Ryson tells Elidir to be wary of Prince Scanlon; quite the opposite."

Ira poured herself a cup of tea, resisting blowing on it to cool it down. Her cousin had a point. Even friendship with the FitzAlcis couldn't be a bad thing. Should she stop teasing her cousin? No. Prince Adeone hadn't shown much interest in anyone, and Nia was in a perfect position to marry him. The daughter of a Lord of Oedran and sister of the Prince's closest friend. There weren't many who had more opportunity to catch his eye.

After a few moments, she said, "So, if you're not betrothed and Festus isn't, I'm hoping there's interesting news somewhere."

Nia grinned. "Well, Festus' little crowd is expanding now Faran's here. If Festus is not with the Prince or avoiding lectures, it's mostly him, Faran and Ifor loitering around the place. Occasionally, Idris will join them. All bemoaning the school. Honestly, it's difficult for a lady to get a dance."

"So, who have you been dancing with?"

Nia shrugged. "I'd much rather hear whom you have."

Ira settled down to tell stories from her time in Garth, touched that Nia listened avidly. The hours passed, with neither of them noticing. Ira struggled to recall all the lessons on deportment that Princess Lilith had instilled in her. She was so comfortable they seemed trivial.

"Do you want lunch served here, girls, or are you joining me?" Her uncle had entered the room without them noticing.

Ira looked up. "Sorry. We're coming." She gave her uncle a restrained hug. "How have you been?"

He slipped an arm around her shoulders. "Far too staid for my niece. The most disastrous thing I've had to deal with was an overturned cart. Admittedly, the escaping chickens did present a bit of a problem, but we didn't let it worry us unduly. How was Garth? How was Her Elegance?"

* * *

After lunch, Ira and Nia rode to Rale House. A footman informed them with a restrained note that Cornelia was in the nursery acting as referee. They made their way upstairs and knocked, listening. They couldn't hear squabbling, so Cornelia had been successful.

When they entered, Aelia flew across the room.

Laughing, Ira swung her into a hug. "You're growing."

Aelia giggled. "Cornelia said I have to listen."

"It's a skill we all need."

Cornelia winked. "If we all listen, who's talking?"

"One of us needs to," admitted Nia. "Where's Finn?"

"I've packed him off to his tutor," replied Cornelia. "He can bother us later. Ae, let Ira sit down."

Ira sank onto a nursing chair and let Aelia sit on her lap, touched the young girl had missed her. "How old are you now?"

"Five!" declared Aelia proudly.

"Hmm. Still ten years younger," teased Ira. "You'll catch me up, eventually."

Whilst Aelia puzzled over that, Cornelia asked Ira if she was ready for Court with all its challenges.

"Possibly. Nia's been telling me you're seeing a lot of Festus."

Cornelia sighed. "Has she? Well, he's asked me to dance a couple of times and that's it. I've seen him at Landis House—"

"When he's missing lectures," muttered Nia.

"...but that's all, and I'm there to visit Nia, not him."

Ira chuckled. "Apparently, he can't marry until Prince Adeone does."

"And Prince Adeone is being tardy about asking Nia," said Cornelia, eyes alight with fun.

Nia blushed. "Not you as well!"

"Everyone's expecting it. Well, everyone in our circle anyway."

Aelia perked up. "Who do you think I'll marry?"

Everyone else exchanged glances. Eventually Cornelia said, "No idea, Ae, but someone who loves you, I hope."

Aelia nodded. "That would be good."

Ira bit her lip. "I just hope I can marry someone I love. Mother was so much younger than father. I'm not sure she got to choose."

Nia became curious. "Why do you say that?"

"A feeling. I think the old King arranged it. Father wouldn't have argued. He never does. What the King says goes."

Cornelia shrugged. "Mine's the same."

"Mine too," admitted Nia carefully. "Though he's not that involved outside of Court."

"Talking of which," said Ira, "any new dances I should know?"

* * *

Ira entered the King's Court wearing her blue silk dress. A few heads turned but no-one stared. That suited her. She wanted to meld into the assembly without fuss. Her father saw her safely with her friends and left them to themselves. They chatted and laughed, eyeing up the younger lords and trying to match them up with friends and acquaintances.

In the Lufian Room, the usher announced the King and they swept into deep curtsies. Ira kept her gaze lowered, hoping he wouldn't notice her. It was a forlorn wish. King Altarius rarely missed anything or anyone that interested him.

"Lady Ira."

Eyes followed her as she crossed to him and swept once more into that deep curtsy. It was more practised than it had been on her first evening at Court around a year before. She'd left for Garth a week later.

"Your Majesty."

"You may rise, my lady. How was our cousin?"

Ira swallowed. "Her Elegance is in perfect health, Sire."

"She certainly had a lot to say about you, Lady Ira. You are most welcome here once more."

As the King moved away, Ira curtsied again, her eyes lowered. Had he seen her uncertainty? If he had, why had he rescued her with the last comment? She returned to her friends, her hand shaking. She wished the whole thing hadn't happened. Everyone was now watching her. Cornelia squeezed her hand.

"You did well."

Ira let her breath out. "Thank you. I wish I was more used to this Court."

"You get used to it," remarked Nia. "Oh no. Go away, Fes."

Festus chuckled. "Sorry, His Highness isn't here yet. Are you surviving the King's attention, cousin?"

"Of course. It's an honour to be noticed by His Majesty." For the first time she could recall, her cousin seemed to be assessing her. He'd opened his mouth to say something when a page appeared and informed him that Prince Adeone was on his way. Ira forestalled him. "Go and play, cousin."

"Play?" muttered Festus without rancour. "One of these days…"

Nia giggled as he left. "How come you get away with teasing him?"

"I don't live with him," replied Ira calmly.

They ambled around Court, chatting amicably. In the great FitzAlcis Chamber, Cornelia let her eyes linger on the murals.

Ira followed her gaze. "They are beautiful."

"Yes. I was thinking that Aelia would love them. She's really taken to drawing. It's all mother can do to get her back to her letters."

"Then get her to illustrate her letters. How is Lady Rale?"

Cornelia smiled. "Well. She'll be pleased to see you. She was visiting Lady Neassa earlier. Oh, did you know Lady Neassa had a boy? They named him Peaga."

"I did. It was family news for Princess Lilith. I believe Her Elegance wrote to Lord Rufus and Lady Neassa. Have Lord Ewart and Lady Amara visited yet?"

"They came at the Munewid, as always," said Nia, "but they didn't stop any longer than normal. Lady Rhian was sorry to have missed you…"

Ira continued listening with one ear. The intricacies of the FitzAlcis family didn't particularly interest her. She had never met Lady Amara since she mostly lived in Tradere with her husband and daughters, daughter now that Neassa was married, she reminded herself. Wasn't there something about a scandal when Lady Amara married Lord Ewart and dropped her title of Princess? Or if not a scandal, a discreet raising of eyebrows that King Altarius had permitted their marriage?

Her attention was caught by Festus entering the room with Prince Adeone. She made an obeisance to the Prince along with everyone else. He might be a prankster, but the King wouldn't take kindly to anyone insulting him. As she straightened up, she looked elsewhere. Catching the Prince's attention wasn't something she desired and he seemed happy to oblige her. When the Prince had passed, Ira said,

"Who was that with them?"

Nia glanced over. "Lord Ifor Daioch. He's all right. Bit provincial, but Festus seems to enjoy his company."

Ira let her attention wander. Lord Ifor wasn't plain, but she wasn't bothered about dancing with him immediately. As she glanced around the Court, she felt oddly out of place. She'd become well acquainted with her peers in Garth, but too many here were strangers. She had the usual gossip about the families of the Lords of Oedran and the ruling FitzAlcis, but outside those groups, she knew next to nothing. Maybe it was time to start a journal, as Princess Lilith had advised.

During the hour before the Court Supper, Lord Faran of Lufian joined them – a ward of the FitzAlcis, who was studying at the Advisors' School, he nonetheless wasn't tied to Prince Adeone's side. Nia and Cornelia welcomed him with smiles, so Ira returned his. She'd met him a couple of times but never to talk with properly.

"Lady Ira, it's lovely to have you in Oedran. Will you favour me with a dance?"

Ira blushed. "If you wish it, my lord, it would be an honour." Faran's standing would help dispel speculation about her early arrival. Not to mention, he was handsome and didn't realise it. What had sent him in her direction? The dance of Court always had purpose even if it appeared meaningless.

Whilst dancing, Lord Faran said, "Festus is glad you're home."

Ira smiled. "Has he been that bad, my lord?"

"In what sense?" enquired Faran. "As far as I'm aware, he's only outraged convention once a week or so."

"Oh dear, I had hoped my absence wouldn't stifle his innovation."

Faran laughed aloud, causing heads to turn in their direction.

Ira blushed. "I'll gain a reputation, my lord, if you continue like that."

Faran chuckled more softly. "My lady, my conscience cannot allow that. Might I beg of you the favour not to make me laugh?"

Ira struggled to contain her merriment. "You can beg, but I'm not sure I can make promises. Her Elegance was certain that a lady never says anything she may have to renege on."

"Garth is rumoured to be a beautiful city."

"Its beauty is rightly renowned, though Oedran has a different grandeur. I love both, but would not swap my home."

Faran smiled. "I too have come to love Oedran, for its architecture, its history and its ladies."

Ira eyed him, amused. "My lord has been studying compliments?"

"That is tomorrow's lesson, Lady Ira."

She laughed, causing more stares. "Lord Faran, your studies progress better than your tutors know. Thank you for the dance of words."

As the music changed, Faran escorted her back to her friends before asking Cornelia for a dance.

Once they were alone, Nia said, "You seemed to enjoy yourself."

"He's better company than I expected. Reminds me of Tyler Galwood. He's going to be a real gentleman in a couple of years. He'll be studying here from next year, so I do wonder what effect this Court will have."

"Do you think he'll stay here in the Palace as Faran has?"

"Only if the King acknowledges the kinship. He doesn't have to. Princess Lilith was very clear with him about that. Shall we wander?"

* * *

By the time she arrived home, Ira was exhausted. The peculiarities of the King's Court had struck her particularly hard by the end of the evening. The only time they were allowed to sit was during the Court Supper. There weren't even chairs in the rooms of Court. If you were lucky, you could sometimes find one of the private rooms empty and sit there, but then rumour and gossip would follow you if you did it too often, especially for younger members of Court. She and her peers were expected to be seen. The Court Supper had also been different and she'd forgotten how sumptuous and filling it could be. There was no pretence. It was a full feast every evening. Tables laden with roast meats, pies and confections spread down each side of the King's Hall with wines, juices and water on tables behind them with servers every four feet tending the needs of two or three courtiers each. It made the Exarch's Court in Garth seem paltry, and that had appeared rich to her when she had settled in. The other peculiarity was that King Altarius preferred the ladies to sit on one side of the hall and the gentleman on the other. There was no chance for fraternisation during the supper. She smiled to herself. It did mean that they could assess each other's charms in different ways. It had been an enjoyable evening, though she hadn't spotted anyone whom she'd like to know better. Watching Festus, Ifor and Faran debating had been amusing when she couldn't hear what they were saying. Festus waving his hands around, Faran's crooked eyebrow and Ifor's quiet smile told her they were teasing him better than hearing the words would have. Further along the table, Idris had been talking with a man whom Nia had informed her was Lord Kenton Parchi, also studying at the School. With them had been an older gentleman whom Cornelia said was Lord Abbas Atgas, visiting for a couple of months as a Guest of Court. Both he and Lord Kenton were from central Anapara. She crossed to her small table and pulled open the drawer. There, she found a piece of parchment and scribbled what she knew on it. That would do. Sleep beckoned. She changed into her nightdress, cursing. She hadn't informed the stables she'd be going for a ride. It would have to be a later ride, for she had no intention of informing them now. Rolling between the covers, she closed her eyes and let the evening's memories lull her into dreams.

Chapter 4
SHOPPING

ALUNADAI DAWNED as Ira slept deeply. Three evenings at Court had taken their toll. The assembly was held into the small hours and started around mid-morning if people wished to attend during the day. She'd been there until Festus and Nia left on all three evenings. They had dropped her off at Macaria House, as her father retired from Court when the King left, or if Prince Adeone stayed later until he did. She half wondered why her father stayed just because the Prince was still there, when he didn't have to, but that was her father and he wasn't alone in it: Lord Iris and Lord Rale did much the same. Other lords would stay for as long as the King did, or beg leave to retire. It made her smile. Surely the King's favour wasn't so easily bought. Princess Lilith, though, had said that the King's favour was never to be relied on, as he could withdraw it without warning.

Waking, Ira rolled onto her back. She needed a day off from the Court. Something peaceful and staid seemed called for. She rang for her maid and asked how long she had until breakfast. On hearing it was half an hour, she cursed. There was no chance for a ride, though that mightn't be a bad thing. After breakfast, she'd sit with Whyte and hear what he needed or didn't need for the garden, then possibly wander along the Maclan.

She sat at the breakfast table looking at the spread of toast, eggs, bacon, jams and juices and didn't want anything. The rich fare of Court had more than satisfied her last night. Knowing her father wouldn't be pleased if she didn't eat, she took a piece of toast and spread it with raspberry jam. Abe had been good to her: there weren't any seeds in the spread. She was licking her fingers in the most unladylike of ways when her father entered.

He sighed. "I thought we'd stopped that habit."

She chuckled. "Sorry, father. I didn't know I would be caught."

"One never does. It's wise, therefore, to not indulge in such habits. What are your plans today?"

"I thought I'd see Whyte about the gardens, then wander along the Maclan. I want to see what new silks Merchant Netherhind has and I need to call by Latimer's and see if he has, or can make me, a journal."

"Why do you need one? I can't think you've any secrets."

Ira smiled. "Every lady has those, father. No. Princess Lilith suggested I keep one detailing whom I meet at Court and where they're from. She says it helps to avoid misunderstandings."

Macaria's lips twitched. "She is right. Talking of Court, I'm presiding today. I'll expect you early in the evening."

"Oh. I'd hoped to have a quiet evening, father."

He pursed his lips. "You will attend whenever I preside. Pick your quiet evenings on other days. It won't be too onerous, but, as you're my heiress, you should be seen on such days. Rather like your mother attended, or Lady Rale attends when Lord Rale presides."

Ira swallowed. She'd forgotten that little tradition. "Of course, father. Will I be required to do anything but be there?"

"No. You simply need to be seen. You won't be seated any higher or need to show favour or displeasure."

"Thank you, father."

He watched her with keen interest. "You might like to know that His Majesty has been impressed with how you've deported yourself over the last few days. I hope you continue in that. I know you are close to Nia, but she can sometimes be too free at Court. Be careful."

Ira hesitated. "She's not indecorous, father."

"No, but she is a Landis," replied her father, as though that explained everything.

Ira chuckled. "It's Festus who says traditions can be changed."

"And young Festus needs to be chary about whom he says that to. Now, if you're going to Latimer's you might see if he has anything you think will suit our library. He knows how we like things bound. Ask him if you can see the new scrolls."

Ira nodded. "Of course, father."

* * *

Ira entered Merchant Netherhind's shop with its bell tinkling. She smiled at the journeyman who moved to greet her. Explaining she was looking for new silks, he showed her their current collection and left her to assess the fabric. The slightly shimmering material held her attention. Should she go with pastel shades or a stronger, deeper colour? She couldn't go with scarlet or emerald as they were the FitzAlcis colours and, anyway, Merchant Netherhind didn't stock them. She settled on a pale blue of a weight to take embroidery. Did she have time to have a dress made and stitched before the Mundimri? It would be close, but— Her mind wandered. Maybe it could wait for the Munewid. Still, the fabric was enticing. She ordered several yards and turned to leave.

"Ira! I thought it was you."

Grinning, Ira looked at the flame-haired girl. "Definitely me. How are you, Leila?"

"Bored. My governess is trying to make me like embroidery. It's not working. I've escaped saying I needed some new fabric."

"She let you come on your own?"

"Not exactly. I've a maid outside but I saw your groom waiting so thought I might actually get some fabric and, that way, I've not lied."

Ira chuckled. "For embroidery?"

"Or a dress. Father wouldn't mind. Will you help me pick?"

They spent several minutes talking. Leila was only a couple of years younger, but the small gap had widened to a gulf now Ira was at Court, along with having been absent for almost a year. Still, after a few minutes, it seemed no time at all had passed.

"Elidir's hardly around to talk to these days," revealed Leila. "Prince Scanlon's taking so much of his time. If he's not at the Palace, then His Highness is at ours. It's annoying me a bit."

"I get the feeling it's often the same with Festus and Prince Adeone. They take all their spare time, but being in favour isn't a bad thing."

"No, it's not, but I want to go for a ride with my brother occasionally, or tease him without having to watch what I say. What do you think about this green?"

"I think it would suit you," said Ira, examining the fern-coloured fabric. "What's Prince Scanlon like?"

Leila's face twitched. "I prefer Prince Adeone. He knows how to have fun. Everyone has to behave exactly right with Prince Scanlon. I hope he loses that. I can't imagine he'll be as kind as Prince Lachlan as Justiciar."

"No. Prince Lachlan's been good for the city," agreed Ira. "How about this one?" She pointed at a pale cream silk.

"Too washed out. I'd better get some linen to needle as well," said Leila nodding to the journeyman. "Master Galdwin, would you find me a lightweight linen that my governess could tolerate?"

The journeyman smiled. "Of course, my lady. Any colour in particular?"

"Not black. I hate stitching on black even more than I hate stitching generally. Thank you. Ira, what do you think of the speculation around Nia?"

Ira shrugged. "I think if we all keep gossiping about it, he'll have to do something."

Leila chuckled. "They'd be so good together! There's a few times we've all dined together, what with Prince Scanlon and Elidir being close and Festus and Prince Adeone being friends. I don't think Prince Adeone's impressed with his brother's attitude but, well, he and Nia are obviously easy in each other's company. It would be so good if they married."

Ira smiled. "There's no telling the future."

Leila sighed. "I'm talking when I shouldn't, aren't I?"

"A bit," admitted Ira, "but I doubt anyone here will say anything."

The journeyman pursed his lips. "Not me, my ladies. I couldn't care less about Court intrigues."

Merchant Netherhind gave a small cough of admonishment.

Ira and Leila shared an amused glance with the journeyman before recollecting themselves.

After a moment, Ira said, "I need to get to Latimer's. Leila, is that all you need here?"

Leila nodded. "Yes. Will you see it delivered, Merchant Netherhind?"

"Of course," said the cloth merchant, giving a slight bow as they left his well-stocked shop.

"Can I come with you to Latimer's?" asked Leila.

"If you want to. It's going to be dull."

"I've the choice between that and embroidery," replied her companion pointedly. "Which do you think I'd rather be doing?"

Ira laughed. "All right. Come on."

They entered the bookseller's still chatting. Wynfeld and Leila's maid waited outside again. Ira watched them talking through the bow-fronted window. They were getting along and part of her felt momentary jealousy. Wynfeld only normally smiled like that with her. Or she thought he had. She reminded herself she hadn't seen him interacting with ladies for a long time.

Latimer crossed to them enquiring how he could help. Explaining what she needed, Ira looked at several pre-made journals, fingering the leaves within them. One felt much smoother than the others.

"What's this one, Merchant Latimer?"

"A new paper, my lady. Made from wood pulp. It's a bit dearer than the other fibres but I do think it's much nicer for writing on."

"I agree. I'd like a thicker journal though."

"I'll have one made up. I'd recommend a maximum of about a hundred leaves. That will give you around two hundred pages."

"Sounds ideal. Thank you. Blue leather, please, and could you add the usual seals into the leather?"

"Of course, my lady. Does it need a year embossing as well? You mentioned it was for a journal."

"No, thank you. It's just for my thoughts rather than as a diary. Leila, have you found anything?"

"I think you should add this to your library," said Leila showing her an illustrated scroll.

Ira burst out laughing. "Why would we need a treatise on beetles?"

"You don't but your father wouldn't be expecting it." Leila's eyes were bright with fun. "Why should our libraries be full of histories?"

"You might have a point." Ira crooked an eyebrow at Merchant Latimer.

"It's a short treatise, my lady. I can get it bound for you. I'm sure His Lordship would appreciate the surprise. In case he doesn't, there's a nice collection of essays on the military tactics of Bayan in the ninth century that is to his more usual taste. Comes from a Bayan historian who has had access to the Citadel archives."

"Sounds ideal," said Ira. "When should we expect the three books?"

"Hopefully by the end of next week, my lady. I'll need to have the paper prepared for your journal. If we complete the others sooner, shall I have them delivered before the journal?"

"Yes, please. Have we settled our last account with you?"

"Yes, my lady. Master Piers was most punctilious about it."

"That's nice to know. Come on, Leila. Let's go and get a drink. Then I think you should probably return home."

An hour later, Leila said, "I wish I could go to Court. It sounds amazing."

"There's sure to be a children's evening soon. Around Prince Scanlon's birthday for sure."

Leila pulled a face. "Yes, but it's not the same, is it? We're just tolerated and everyone watches what they say."

"Until you're fifteen, it's the only time you're permitted to attend."

Leila pouted. "It's not fair. You, Cornelia and Nia can all go."

"Aelia can't."

"She's five!"

"True," admitted Ira. "It's not that long until you're fifteen."

"It's two years!" retorted Leila. "It's ages."

"It'll pass quickly," replied Ira quietly. "Honestly, Leila, it does pass more quickly than you realise. Cornelia was there a couple of years before me, and I felt like you do, but it soon went."

"I suppose so," said Leila. "So, what's this about Tyler Galwood being a proper gentleman to you?"

Ira blushed. "He was kind and attentive, but he's not at Court yet."

"Would you marry him?"

"Leila Ryson, honestly, you're absolutely incorrigible. I doubt it will even be mooted. I can't marry someone who'll inherit his own title. I need to marry a second son and avoid a fortune hunter."

"That won't be easy. Everyone knows you're your father's heiress."

"So they do. Who do you think you'll marry? The Teran lads are about your age, Tyron in particular. Then there's Finn—."

"Urgh, no! It'd be like marrying my brother."

Ira laughed. "Talking of which, you really should be getting home before your governess or father sends out a search party."

Leila sighed. "Thanks for the tea and company. It's nice to know you've not become all grand in Garth."

Chapter 5
LETTERS
Septadai, Week 20 – 28th Meithal, 14th Meithis 1193
Macarian House

AN ALUNA-MONTH LATER, life had settled into a predictable routine of
Court, rides and household duties. Ira had hosted her friends for evenings
and accepted invitations in return. At least she could include Leila in those.
Writing the previous evening's gleanings in her journal, Ira realised it was
helping her in ways she hadn't expected. Not only was she learning about
her fellow courtiers but she had more to talk to them about should their paths
cross. She was retaining the information all the better for it. She'd called
again at Latimer's for a second journal. He'd hid his curiosity well, but it
still made her smile. She'd add her fellow courtiers to their own pages, at
least for those giving her a lot to write about. She kept the journals, and her
completion of them, private. There was no need for her friends to know.
Her memory impressed them and they jokingly said it must be because she
had a star stone in the family. The mythical stones were meant to hold and
generate magic. One of twelve that had existed, her family's most valuable
jewel hardly saw the light of day or, for that matter, the candles of Court.
Her father kept it in a secure box, in a secure chest, in a secure vault, and
she'd only seen it twice. Once, exasperated, her father had shown it her to
prove it existed and the second time she'd worn it for her first evening at
Court. Keeping it secure was important, but did it render owning it pointless?

She walked downstairs for lunch, having checked all the bedrooms except
her father's to make sure the maids were actually cleaning them. She didn't
want unexpected guests to find dusty rooms.

Crossing the hallway, she glanced at the side table and noted several
letters lay waiting. Two were for her father, but his study door had been
closed, so disturbing him was probably best avoided. Three were for her
and she recognised the writing immediately. All were from Bayan. Two
from friends she had made and the last was from Princess Lilith. She
picked it up thoughtfully. Should she eat first? No. It had taken weeks to
arrive. She crossed to the drawing room, carefully weighing the letter in her
hand. It would tell her why she'd been sent home, give her some reassurance,
advise on a remedy for any insult. With her heart beating faster than
normal, she broke the seal.

My dearest Ira,
Please let me assure you that you have nothing to
apologise for. Quite the reverse. Your behaviour during your
visit was nothing but impeccable, your deportment both at

home and Court was a joy to watch and your love of life a welcome lift to our souls. If I could explain how different it has seemed here since you left, I am sure you would not believe me.

I feel I must now apologise to you. Your visit was arranged by your father and His Majesty during your 14th year. Knowing your family was small, it was a pleasure to bring you into mine for even a short time. As a Guest of Court here, we all hoped that your stay would be enjoyable and long. As time passed, I saw something more in you. We could have found you a husband amongst our second sons, I have little doubt about that, but that wasn't you, my dear. At least, it's not you here.

I believed, and still do, that your future lies in our wonderful home city. The King's Court is varied and brimming with eligible lords, all tripping over themselves with ambition, but not all bad. I am certain amongst the courtiers is a voice that will make your soul sing. Your friends were obviously missing your company and you theirs. It seemed selfish of me to keep you in Garth any longer than necessary.

You cannot meet your future if you are seen as anything but a lady in possession of her own heart and mind. In that, you have never wavered or failed. You are ready for the King's Court in a way I've rarely seen. I am just sorry I didn't explain this to you before you left. I never meant to cause you any angst and am always your friend,

Princess Lilith Fitz Alcis

Ira folded the letter carefully, put it on the table by her chair, wiping her eyes with the back of her hand. She hadn't been 'sent away'. She hadn't done anything wrong. Anything to fear over. The relief was overwhelming. It didn't explain her father's coldness, but maybe he hadn't known the reasons. Princess Lilith might just have written that she was on her way home. It wouldn't be unusual and if the messenger had taken the Oaks Ridge road as opposed to the Shinglis one, the letter would have reached Oedran well ahead of her.

"Are you lunching, Ira?"

She closed her eyes before pushing herself to her feet. "Sorry, father. I'm coming."

His gaze raked across her. "What's upset you?"

"Nothing. Her Elegance wrote back."

"So?"

She passed him the letter. It was easier than explaining.

"Why were you crying?" he asked when he'd finished reading it.

"Relief, I suppose."

He gave a short nod. "Learn to control those emotions."

As they left for the dining room, Ira wondered idly if she could do anything right. Keeping her emotions in check was not the start and end of everything. She was in her own home. At Court she wouldn't have even read the letter. The response annoyed her so much she didn't say a word over lunch. It was safer.

After lunch, she broke the seals on her other correspondence. Her Bayan friends were missing her presence and hoped she was enjoying being home and at the King's Court, which they wanted to know all about. She smiled to herself and drew out parchment and pen to reply to all of them. Whilst she was at it, she penned a brief letter to Tyler Galwood. She hoped when he arrived in Oedran to study at the school, he could live at the Palace where there were at least Faran and Adeone to keep him company if the Prince enjoyed his company, that was. Idly, she toyed with her pen before sealing the letter thoughtfully. Two minutes later, she was in her father's study saying,

"Father, could Tyler Galwood live here whilst he studies at the Advisors' School? It would be nice to return the Galwoods' hospitality."

Her father eyed her. "Is that all?"

"Yes. He and his family were very kind to me and I feel like it would be an acceptable gesture."

"I'll speak to the King. It will depend on His Majesty, as Lord Galwood is part of his family."

Ira nodded. "But Tyler isn't, not legally. It's only to the great-grandchild of a king and Tyler's a generation below that."

"It's still a decision for His Majesty; however, I'm sure he'll be touched you've thought about it."

Ira left the study idly contemplating if every conversation that included a man would end up with questions about her marriage. Was that all she was now? A wife-to-be. She should have expected it. All the conversations she and her friends had revolved around who they'd marry, or who their friends would marry. Would every discussion in later years revolve around their children? There had to be more to life than that. She wanted to ride, read, help others, not simply be a wife and mother.

Frustrated, she went to the stables.

Seeing her mood, Jack sat her on a bale of hay, passing her a mug of stewed tea and an apple. "What's caught your thoughts, m'lady?"

"Something I'd rather not think about. Where's Lex?"

"Out. Sent him to the farrier. Why?"

"Oh, I fancied a gallop and he'll let me. Everyone else tries to stop me."

Jack chuckled. "For good reason, m'lady. Anyway, does he 'let you' or do you just not give him any choice?"

Her lips twitched. "Maybe. Jack, why can't I be who I want to be?"

He shrugged. "No-one can, m'lady. We all have dreams that we wake up from. I don't hate my life, but, as a lad, I wanted something beyond stable work. Never got it. Was even left here in sixty-nine. His Lordship didn't want me with him in Bayan, so I had to stop here."

Ira picked at the hay. "You'd have liked to fight?"

"Nah. I'd have liked to have travelled. Seen a bit of the empire. The fighting, well, I ain't good with a sword. Probably best I had to stay here. Too many died because lords wanted more."

"Yes. There's still no city gates in Garth."

"Good job too," said Jack. "That rebellion cost us all dear." He took her hand. "Don't dwell on what can't be changed, little Ira. Just make what's left what you want it to be."

She met his gaze. "How long will Lex be?"

Jack sighed. "I should send you off with a different groom."

Her lips twitched. "You wouldn't do that to them in my mood."

He snorted. "You may have a point, m'lady. I'll saddle your mare and a horse for him. He shouldn't be long."

Ira put her empty mug down. "You are too good to me, Jack."

He chuckled. "Ah, it's nothing. You go and get changed and I'll sort the horses and send word when the lad's back."

The gallop freed up her mind as she'd hoped. Beside her, Wynfeld chuckled at her grin and the way she lifted her face to the autumn breeze. She caught his amusement and pouted.

"It's nice to be out. Father's not been too encouraging today."

"He'll be saving it for tomorrow, my lady."

"I hope so. I don't want him to spoil my birthday. Do you know if anything's planned?"

Wynfeld crooked an eyebrow. "Why would I? I'm only a groom."

"You definitely know something. Come on, tell."

"More than my life's worth. Aunt Maria has a sharp hand."

"Maria's a softy," replied Ira. "With a sharp hand, admittedly."

They both laughed before Wynfeld said, "Do you remember the time I climbed the apple tree and then helped you up?"

"Hardly likely to forget the scolding I received."

"I had a thrashing from your father and a scolding from my aunt. The latter was worse."

Ira paused. "I didn't realise that. I'm sorry."

"What for?" asked Wynfeld, perplexed.

"All of it. I encouraged you to do it."

"I didn't have to agree and it was worth it." He chuckled. "Seeing you sitting next to me in the tree, eating an apple, is a memory I'll always have. It was worth every bit of what came after."

She smiled ruefully. "I'm glad, but I'm still sorry father thrashed you."

He shrugged. "I shouldn't encourage the lady of the house to act like a stable lad, apparently. It's a shame that the lady of our house knows more about horses than most stable boys."

"Speaking from experience," quipped Ira. "Jack was a good teacher. I sometimes wonder if I'd have had such a varied childhood if mother had lived." She reined in her mare and dismounted. Seeing Wynfeld's face, she rolled her eyes. "I want to walk for a bit."

"Fine. Just don't climb any trees."

Ira's laughter pealed through the woodland's rustles. "I won't."

Wynfeld dismounted. They led their horses along the path, reminiscing about misdemeanours they'd encouraged each other to. The past was safe. There were no thoughts of the future, of marriage or children. As they led their horses out of the woodland, Wynfeld stopped, patting her mare gently, coaxing her into lifting her hoof. It was clear her shoe was loose.

"You can't ride her, my lady. Let me swap the saddles over."

Ira shook her head. "It's already late. It will take too long. Can I ride pillion with you?"

Wynfeld let out a long breath. "You could, but I don't know what your father would say."

Ira shrugged. "To the city gates then. It'll be quicker. We can both walk home from there. It's not that far."

He pursed his lips.

"Lex, come on. You know I'm right."

"I'm not meant to say if you're not." He lifted her up behind his saddle. Taking her mare's reins, he swung into his saddle with familiar ease.

Ira slipped her arms around him. It had been years since they'd been this close and he tensed slightly before relaxing. She rested her head between his shoulder blades.

"I need a bit more freedom of movement, my lady."

She moved her head. Had she imagined the catch in his voice? As they returned to the city gates, her breathing deepened. She had finally relaxed properly. There was no talk, no laughter, no reminiscing, and yet, she was calmer than she had been in days, weeks, even. When they reached the gates, Wynfeld dismounted and took her waist to help her alight. Their eyes met for a moment longer than felt safe.

Both feet firmly on the paved street, she thanked him, saying for the gate guards' benefit. "We should take her straight to the farrier."

On reaching Macarian House, Jack eyed the pair of them. "I shouldn't let you out, you know."

They chuckled.

"This wasn't my fault, Jack," said Ira. "She almost lost a shoe. We had to take it steady coming back."

"Aye, well. Get yourself inside. Your father's been asking after you." As Ira left, she heard him say, "What happened, lad? No, not with the mare."

She bit her lip. Was it obvious? Nothing had happened. They had shared a glance. One full of meaning that neither of them had realised was there but it had only been a glance. She dressed for Court rather more carefully than normal and in a much quieter frame of mind, picking jewels she seldom wore. The sparkle of the diamonds against the blue silk did take the eye. She took the brooch off. It wasn't the night for drawing attention. She caught sight of herself in the mirror and looked away. Lex wasn't her future. He was her childhood friend. She sank onto her bed. Was he just her childhood friend? Her companion. She'd never really talked about him to anyone, she realised. Not even Festus and Nia. Whenever they'd called round, he'd been sent elsewhere and she'd learned not to talk about him. Had she ever mentioned him? She didn't think so and now it seemed odd to. Even when Festus had seen her riding he hadn't noted it was Wynfeld. He'd referred to him as her 'escort'. She turned the brooch over in her hands, ambivalent to its glints. His hands at her waist had stirred something, and he'd been so deliberate, so certain, no hesitancy at all. She shook herself. It was one moment, one small moment, it meant nothing. He meant nothing. A friend, yes, but nothing more. She put the brooch away and went downstairs to meet her father. She had to attend Court, not a world of dreams.

Chapter 6
BIRTHDAY

MARIA WOKE HER the following day with breakfast in bed. Ira hugged her by return. The indulgence was welcome, and she sank back into her pillows with a grin.

"So what's planned for today?"

Maria chuckled. "Why would anything be planned? Anyway, shouldn't you know as mistress of the household?"

Ira snorted. "You know that this is one day father doesn't let me manage anything. He schemes it all out and pretends he's done nothing and it's all a big surprise to him."

"He loves you, little Ira."

"I know, and I him; however, my question still stands. What's planned?"

"A ride, for starters."

Ira shook her head. "Not this morning. I think the gallop yesterday was enough."

Maria's eyes narrowed. "What happened?"

"Nothing! But my mare has a loose shoe for a start."

"Well, if nothing happened, you can go for that ride."

Ira sighed. "So what's going to surprise me when I get home?"

Maria smiled. "There might have been invitations for lunch."

"Then I'll have a quiet morning up here and you can do whatever you need to when I should have been on that ride. In fact, could I have an indulgent bath?"

Maria's eyes narrowed. "I'll see if there's enough water heated. What shall I tell your father?"

Ira shrugged. "My course is early."

"You want *me* to tell your father *that?*"

"Fine. Tell him I'm having women's troubles then. It amounts to the same thing. He's been married. He knows how these things work."

Maria chuckled. "True. You enjoy your breakfast then, and I'll sort everything else out."

* * *

Ira wallowed in the bath, enjoying the enveloping warmth and scents of Serpent Isle sandalwood. Indulgent wasn't a strong enough word and she didn't care. This was her time. A year ago she'd known she'd be leaving for Garth, and there had been the trepidation over that and being presented at Court. Two years ago, she'd been fretting to be a year older. This year, this year was her year. She might not have her future worked out, but at least she wasn't waiting for the next stage. She paused. Wasn't she? She had spent the month since returning constantly talking about marriage. Yet it hadn't been about her own marriage. She'd been teasing Nia and Cornelia, speculating about Festus, Faran and Ifor, but not seriously considering her own future. Why? Why had she avoided that question?

She breathed in deeply. All right. It was a new year, a new start. She had to be honest with herself. Did she want to marry? Was that the right question? Could she stay single? No. She was the last of the Macaria line. Her father would want her to continue it, and the spectres of her ancestors loomed large. She had to at least try to continue their legacy. Even if she declared she didn't want to marry, as Lady Rhian Fairson had, she doubted she'd be permitted the choice. She wasn't yet an adult. Such choices weren't in her control. It wasn't fair. Lex, being cisan, was already considered an adult. She had four more years before she would be, and yet there was only a year's difference between her and Lex. She paused, reaching for the soap. What had happened yesterday? Had her heart raced, or had she imagined it? She still felt his hands at her waist. When was the last time he'd touched her before that? It must be years ago. Climbing the apple tree? Probably. Had her father truly beaten him for her mischief? She closed her eyes. Their laughter cut across the years. A smile crept into her heart and onto her lips. How often had they encouraged each other? Climbing up behind the stables, playing hide and seek around the house, learning to ride, learning to dance... She drew a sharp breath, longing for the carefree hours. When Lex had started working properly, their hours together had become limited, but there'd still been the rides and the odd sneaked evening. Maria and her father had turned a blind eye. Longing for the carefree evenings wouldn't bring them back. She needed to stop living in the past. Lex was a childhood friend, that was all. Yesterday was an aberration. They'd been laughing, reminiscing, thinking of times when they could be freer. They couldn't be that free now. Her stomach plummeted. Why? Why couldn't they? What was so bad if she cared for someone, anyone? Love wasn't finite. It didn't know rank or position. Why couldn't she care about others? For others? Drinking in the aroma of sandalwood once more, she paid heed to all her feelings. She had to stop thinking like this. She ached, and not just in her heart. Pulling herself out of the bath, she wrapped a towel around herself. She had to dress for entertaining, though she wasn't sure who was visiting. Close friends and family were the likeliest, so she could be freer than with her Court clothes. She picked a purple bodice that was fitted to her curves, petticoats that would give the matching skirt a bit of body, and a silver and diamond necklace that would match the silver-toned embroidery. The bodice wasn't low cut, but she'd never have worn it to Court, for it was too fitted for the fashion there. Her father wouldn't be pleased if she drew the wrong sort of attention before she was betrothed, if not married. The fact that attention might get her a husband was simply irony. Why did she have to find her husband at Court anyway? The King hadn't found his last wife there. She sighed, looking at herself in the mirror. She didn't hate all the rules for her life. They did mean she didn't have to agonise over her decisions. Those clear set rules helped all of them, but why shouldn't she wonder about other options. She swung her hips slightly making the skirt swish freely and giggled. There was still something so childish about enjoying the movement but she loved it.

Maria entered as she was giggling and crooked an eyebrow. "Next, you'll twirl on the spot."

Ira did. "What do you think?"

Maria pretended to consider. "You're still you. Even at sixteen."

Ira giggled again. "Good." She turned to the mirror. "Time to grow up, though, isn't it? In Garth I felt much more of a lady than I do here."

Maria spun her around. Holding Ira's gaze, she said, "You are a lady your mother would be proud of, little Ira. You don't have to be composed to be kind, you don't have to be calm to be ladylike. Admittedly, you do need to keep your feet on the ground and remember your manners, but you can still enjoy life."

Ira gave her old nurse a hug. "You can't imagine how much I missed you in Garth."

"Your letters hinted," replied Maria with a soft smile. "Now, there's a few people downstairs. Do I need to continue lying for you?"

"No. I'm coming. I've enjoyed this morning."

* * *

Ira stepped off the last stair with a grin at her father and Festus, who were waiting patiently. Both gave her the day's greetings, but there was a restraint she hadn't expected. They must have seen her hesitation because Festus said,

"It's nothing to worry about."

"What isn't?" she asked suspiciously.

"Me," stated a voice with a wry note.

She glared at her cousin before turning and curtsying. "Your Highness." It was all she could think of to say. Why was Prince Adeone at her birthday celebrations?

"May I offer Your Ladyship the day's blessings? I hope you don't mind, but I didn't let Festus escape without explanation and I wanted to wish you the best myself."

Before she could reply, her father had said, "You're most welcome here, Your Highness. I am sure I speak for my daughter as well."

"Of course, father. It's an honour to have you in our home, sir."

Prince Adeone's lips twitched. "Thank you. I shouldn't stop the day's festivities. Nia and I were in the middle of a debate."

Ira watched him enter the drawing room and crooked an eyebrow at her cousin, who pulled a face.

"Blame me later. Are you joining us, Uncle Macaria?"

"I will for lunch. I know better than to interfere in your nattering. Unless His Highness asks where I am, I'll be in my study."

"Won't you be there anyway?" enquired Festus innocently. "Should the Prince ask for you, I will deliver the message. Ow." He rubbed his head where his uncle had clipped him.

Ira laughed. "That serves you right." She turned to enter the drawing room and squealed as Festus grabbed her. "Will you stop doing that!"

"Not a chance. Well, not today." He added in a whisper, "Happy birthday. You look beautiful."

She glanced over her shoulder at him and smiled her thanks as she crossed the threshold of the drawing room. Her gaze took in the sight of her friends sitting together. Not just those from Court but those who were too young to attend. Cornelia and Nia were talking to Adeone, who had sat Aelia on his lap. Faran, Ifor Daioch, Elidir Ryson and Finn Rale were playing cards. Leila was trying to help Finn, who was muttering that he didn't need her help. Amused, Ira gave a brief bob in Adeone's direction and went and tickled Finn out of his chair.

"I was going to say happy birthday," he grouched.

Ira laughed. "Are you too upset with me to sit next to me?"

"No, but there's no space."

"Oh, isn't there? Then you'll have to sit on me then."

He chuckled. "I'm too big now. I was losing anyway. Leila *helped*."

"She plays better than you do, Finn."

"No, she doesn't," he muttered. "She cheats!"

"What me?" asked Leila innocently. "It wasn't my fault that Lord Faran didn't notice the mirror over his shoulder and you're too honourable."

Faran glanced over his shoulder, groaning. "I appreciate your honesty, Finn. We'll restart the game on a level."

"But Finn didn't cheat," remarked Leila. "Oh, happy birthday, Ira. I like your dress. The colour is wonderful."

Ira returned the compliment and watched as Ifor dealt cards and Finn settled himself on the floor. A few minutes later, she and Leila were both throwing in helpful comments, which had their friends threatening dire retribution. After a while, Ira suggested she and Leila went for a walk in the gardens. It seemed a simple way of keeping the peace and getting out of the Prince's way. It wasn't that he was being intrusive; he was just there, and she couldn't relax. He hadn't even looked in her direction, but she knew he was present. As she and Leila crossed to the door into the gardens, Cornelia joined them. Did she also want to get out of the Prince's presence?

The gardens were cool, but not unpleasant. Ira led the way down the path in silence until they were well out of hearing of the house.

"I'm going to kill Festus."

Cornelia chuckled. "No, you're not. He can't refuse if His Highness wants to accompany him somewhere."

"Why today though?" grumbled Ira. "I was having a lovely day."

Leila frowned. "Why don't you like His Highness?"

"I just…" Ira considered. "I find him distant. He looks right through me."

"Bit difficult in that dress," replied Cornelia with a smile.

"Oh, no. He'll—" Ira stopped abruptly. "I should go and change."

Cornelia slipped her arm through Ira's, imprisoning her on the spot. "No, you shouldn't. You look lovely and this is your home. So what if it's not a Court dress? Last time I checked, none of us are dressed formally."

Ira pulled a face. "I'm the hostess—"

Leila took her other arm. "We can wrestle you to the ground if you don't stop talking nonsense."

"Your deportment lessons are working then," said Ira, her eyes twinkling.

Leila laughed. "Sorry. I wish I could wear a dress like yours. I don't have the curves."

"They'll come. If not, the right stays can work wonders." Ira looked at the house. Her father was watching her with an easily read frown. He thought she should be inside entertaining the Prince. Well, the Prince was entertained enough by Festus and Nia and had invited himself. He would cope without her for a time. They continued the amble. She was in no hurry to return to the stifling room.

A few minutes later, they turned back towards the house and Ira caught sight of the apple tree in the distance. She giggled. Cornelia caught her eye.

"What did we say?"

Ira shook her head. "Nothing. Honestly, it was nothing you said. It was a memory surfacing."

Leila once more slipped her arm through Ira's. "Do tell us what it was."

"I don't think that would be a good idea," replied Ira, her eyes still alight with fun.

"Is it a secret?" asked Cornelia. "Maybe a forbidden kiss."

"It's not that!" exclaimed Ira. As her friends teased her, trying to draw the memory from her, she considered. Why couldn't she tell them? The incident wasn't recent and she didn't have to mention Lex. "Fine," she said, laughing. "I once climbed the apple tree. I was remembering sitting on the bough munching away."

Cornelia snorted in the most unladylike way possible. "You did what?"

"I climbed the apple tree," said Ira, laughing again, eyes bright with the memory. "It was just something I wanted to do." She became wistful. "I would never do it now."

"Can I?" asked Leila. "I'm going to try." She ran off.

Ira cursed and gave chase, laughing. "Leila, you can't—"

Both of them stopped abruptly. Festus and Adeone were on the terrace, watching them. Ira gave her best Court curtsy, whilst Leila simply bobbed and went to run off again.

Festus caught her. "What are you up to?"

"Climbing the apple tree," said Leila. "Ira once did."

The blood rushed to Ira's face. "Years ago!"

"So you're far too old for such things, Leila," said Festus. "Your brother is asking for you."

Leila sighed. "It would be fun though."

"I'm sure it would," replied Festus, "but lunch is ready. We just came to tell you."

Ira had been watching them, but was aware that the Prince had been watching her, ignoring Festus and Leila. Her face was still hot and his gaze inflamed her even more, but she couldn't ask him to stop staring. She took a deep breath.

"We should dine, if that suits Your Highness."

Adeone inclined his head slightly. "Of course. Anything for someone who can climb trees."

He was making fun of her and the story would be all around the Court in hours. It would not impress her father.

"Can I request a birthday favour, Your Highness?"

His eyes twinkled. "Of course."

"Can you not tell this story to *anyone*?"

He laughed. "I wouldn't dare refuse Your Ladyship that. Might I escort you to lunch?"

She took his proffered arm. She shouldn't have requested the favour. He'd find a different way to tell the story. If the King found out, she dreaded to think what would happen. He would say something to her father, she was sure about that, and then there'd be more trouble.

Lunch was a more subdued meal than it might have been. Her father rightfully tried to give the Prince the place of honour.

Adeone laughed. "Not today, Macaria. It's Lady Ira's day. I'll sit right at the bottom. I'm uninvited and here for selfish reasons."

She took her seat, perplexed.

Elidir, who was almost ten, frowned. "What reason is that, sir?"

Macaria pursed his lips. "We do not ask princes for their reasons, Elidir."

"I'm sorry, Your Highness," apologised the young boy.

Adeone winked at him. "Escaping my duties and tutor. I expect my brother is no different on occasion."

Elidir hesitated. "His Highness is dedicated, sir."

Macaria opened his mouth to remonstrate. A glare from Adeone closed it.

"One of us has to be," said the Prince. "Sit with me and tell me what you've been doing."

Ira inwardly applauded. The Prince had outmanoeuvred her father with very few words and a glance. Adeone and Elidir had an easy relationship. How often did they see each other? It must be frequent with how unfazed Elidir was.

Beside her, Festus said, "You're quiet."

She caught his eye. "Are you surprised?"

"A bit," he admitted. "I'm not used to it."

Her lips twitched. "I'm now a lady."

Festus purposefully looked puzzled. "You are? All right, all right, I'm sorry. You are," he finished lamely. "Are you coming to Court later?"

Ira shook her head. "I hadn't planned to. I wondered if you, Cornelia and Nia fancied a quiet evening, where we can sit and talk."

She didn't miss Festus' darting glance at Adeone, who seemed deep in conversation with Nia and Leila.

"I'll see what happens after lunch. If His Highness is called away, I might manage it."

After lunch, they returned to the drawing room, all nicely full with roast chicken, rich gravy, crispy potatoes and batter puddings. For dessert, there'd been a decadent lemon meringue on a biscuit base, Ira's favourite.

She sank into her usual chair without thinking and hastily pushed herself back to her feet. "My apologies, Your Highness."

He laughed. "I can cope, Lady Ira. I understand the wish. Your cook does good meals." He sat down beside her, nodding for her to resume her place.

She did so, saying, "Father found him in one of the cooks' tents during the rebellion. Comes from the Rex Dallin originally. I believe his youngest brother works at Ceardlann in the kitchens." She couldn't think of anything else to say. Should she know that much about a servant? Would it look like she didn't appreciate her allotted place? It was too late now to retract the words but she flushed nonetheless.

Adeone frowned, which didn't help her unease, but it seemed he was only thinking. "Hmm. I wonder if it's Marnin. I certainly recognise that lemon meringue."

Ira smiled. "It's my favourite, sir. I only get it on my birthday."

"Then I hope he's made one for you for later as well."

She saw the way he studied her face and the flush returned.

He chuckled. "You blush easily, my lady."

"She does," said Festus, "though we try not to make her uncomfortable mentioning it, sir."

"His Highness is entitled to—" she began.

"No, I'm not," said Adeone quickly. "I'm not entitled to make anyone uncomfortable on their day. You have my apologies, my lady. I hope you can forgive me."

"Of course, Your Highness."

"No, not forgive the Prince. Forgive *me* for the blundering idiot I am."

Ira didn't get a chance to reply before her cousin said, "Traditions can be changed."

She laughed before she'd considered her reaction. "Festus! You're incorrigible."

"We're in agreement there," stated Adeone. "Though I'm not sure if it was the tradition of forgiveness or blundering idiocy that can be changed."

"There's nothing like ambiguity, sir," replied Festus innocently.

"Tell me, Lady Ira, have you any technique to manage him?"

"I tell him it's time for him to go home, sir."

"Does it work?"

"Occasionally, sir. If I want a quiet evening, I find avoidance best."

Festus' eyes narrowed, but she smiled sweetly at him. He stuck out his tongue and then recalled himself.

"Now you're blushing, Festus," said Adeone, lips twitching.

By the time her friends began to excuse themselves, Ira had relaxed more than she expected. The Prince had been courteous and teasing in equal measure, but, amongst her closest circle, teasing was part of life. When he said he ought to be going, she pushed herself to her feet.

"No, my lady, don't bother yourself. I'll take my leave of your father whilst they saddle my horse. I hope to see you at Court later."

She cursed in the privacy of her head. "Of course, Your Highness."

"Good. Festus, don't worry about accompanying me. I've taken too much of your time already. I'll see you this evening." With that he left.

Ira waited for the door to close before crooking an eyebrow at her cousin.

"He's not looked right through you today," replied Festus.

"You... You're... Argh."

"Expressive as ever, Ira. Will you be at Court?"

"How can I now avoid it?" she muttered. "The *Prince* hopes to see me there. I can just imagine the reaction if I don't turn up."

"All right. I'm sorry. I didn't realise it would cause so much trouble."

She sighed. "Oh, never mind. I guess I can't avoid Court every birthday."

Chapter 7
DANCING
Evening
Macarian House – Study

HER FATHER CALLED HER into his study after the Prince left and held out a gold trinket box, its blue sapphires glinting in the light.

"It's time you claimed it, little Ira."

She opened the lid. There, on a bed of silver velvet, glinted the cabochon cut blue star stone. A sapphire but with a depth of colour she'd never seen in another stone. She'd have to find a gown to do it justice. Until then… She caught her father's eye.

"Why?"

"You're right. It should be worn. Just be careful of it. Wear it tonight. It's your birthday."

She smiled sadly. "I'm sorry I've not seen much of you."

He wrapped her in a rare hug. "It's been an upside-down day. His Highness mentioned seeing us at Court later. I think we should attend."

Ira bit her lip. "I said we would when he asked. I didn't know how to refuse. I'm sorry if—"

"You did the right thing. I know you don't always understand why we have to be at their beck and call so much, but I want you to inherit without challenge. If they know us, know you, it'll be harder for them to refuse you your inheritance."

"Do you think they would?"

He shrugged and sank onto his chair. "It's been known. I trust the King would abide by my wishes as a man, but as King it's trickier for him. He has to think of the empire and its stability. The consequences of the Bayan Rebellion will outlive us all. Tradition, no matter what that wed-nephew of mine says, cannot always be changed."

Ira knelt by him. "It's tradition I should inherit."

"No, it's not. It's ancient Macian law. Our ancestors were allowed to bring it with them to the Lordship of Oedran, but that doesn't mean the FitzAlcis couldn't renege on the agreement. Given the hundreds of years in the way, I don't think there'd be trouble and they might need to placate more powerful people than you, little Ira."

She rested her head on his hand. "I have to stop being a child then."

"You stopped that many moons ago."

She studied his face. "Did I? Not in my heart. I still want to run and laugh and gallop carefree. I can act the part, but I don't feel it inside."

"All of life is an act, Ira. None of us feels the age we are. Though I am starting to."

"Well, our ancestors are going to have to do without you for longer because I need you here."

He laughed. "I'm not going anywhere yet. Go and get changed. Take the stone."

She changed from her purple dress into the blue silk. The slightly looser fit was better for Court and the dress was comfortable and familiar. It's colour, which had seemed rich before, paled against the star stone. Maybe she'd take the stone to Master Netherhind for advice on the right fabric. Until then, the dress was the best she had for the stone.

She was quiet in the coach. There was something unnerving about the evening. Was it because she hadn't thought she'd be attending? Or was it the stone? Was it somehow affecting her mood? She wanted to ask her father if they could leave early, but it wouldn't be possible. He would have to stay for the Court Supper, which meant staying until the King retired at the earliest. If the King wasn't there, then until Prince Adeone did and he seldomly retired early.

They gave their names to the clerk recording attendance. Why they had to was a mystery to her, but she supposed it helped someone somewhere start to predict what would be needed. Those heads that did turn as they entered soon turned back, but one or two lingered on her, noticing the stone. Festus crossed to greet them with a slight inclination of his head to her father. Who to make an obeisance to at Court, and who not to, was one of its many complexities. She wondered how the men remembered it all. For the women it was relatively simple. There was a structure, and woe betide anyone who overstepped the mark with Lady Amara, but it wasn't as strict once beyond the FitzAlcis and Ladies of Oedran.

Festus grinned. "It's been let out."

Macaria crooked an eyebrow meaningfully. "To what or whom are you referring, young Festus?"

"The star stone, Uncle Macaria. We hardly ever see it."

"Well, it's now Ira's, so she may take pity on you more often. Though, I rather suspect not. I'll leave you to your wrangles. Is your father here?"

Festus nodded. "In the Tradere room, sir."

Ira watched him leave. "You're here early."

Festus shrugged. "Didn't seem much point to waiting about at home and the Prince had things to attend to that didn't require me. He enjoyed today." Festus lowered his voice. "He likes informality away from here."

Her brows knitted. "Why tell me that now?"

"Because I think you need to know it," said Festus. "There's no escaping his acquaintance now you're at Court permanently and he's our age, so you're going to bump into him with me and Nia, not to mention Cornelia, Faran and Ifor."

Ira bit at her lip. "He'll not take any notice of me."

"Won't I, my lady?" asked Adeone from behind her. "Would you like a dance?"

Ira glared at her cousin, wishing looks could inflict pain before turning, curtsying and accepting the dance.

"Don't blame your cousin," whispered Adeone. "I made sure I wasn't announced. I like to catch him out."

"Me too, sir. I hope I didn't cause offence."

"No offence at all. You spoke the truth. You're good at that."

She swallowed. "Thank you, sir." How did he know what she was good at? Had Festus been talking behind her back? She hardly thought about the dance at all. It was only after it had ended and Adeone had returned with her to their friends that she realised he'd been silent as well. He collected Ifor with a look and left.

Ira rounded on Festus. "Did you know he was behind me?"

"Only when it was too late to warn you."

"It's the last time we're that close to a door," muttered Ira.

Cornelia smiled. "Let's amble, Ira. You need to show off that stone and Festus needs to play elsewhere."

"I do?" asked Festus, confused.

"Before Ira forgets she's at Court," replied Nia. "Come on, brother, you can dance with me."

"I get all the treats," mumbled Festus, grinning.

"That or the blame," replied Cornelia.

Faran on the sidelines was chuckling to himself. "You two are like an old married couple already."

Everyone turned to him.

"Just saying."

Ira chuckled. "Will you join us on our amble, my lord?"

"I shall, Lady Ira. Thank you."

An hour later, they were back in the FitzAlcis Chamber when Faran gave a slight bow and moved aside. Ira turned to find Adeone beside her once again, once again asking for a dance. This time, she heard the murmurs and whispers that followed them.

Beside her Adeone said, "Ignore them, my lady. It's your birthday. Their gossip is not our business."

"Unless father gets to hear it, sir," she replied carefully.

"I'll sort out Macaria," he stated in a voice that made her remember his position far too clearly.

"We would not like to inconvenience Your Highness."

"I wouldn't like to think my actions have caused you issues, my lady."

"It's very thoughtful of you, sir. Thank you."

"Next you'll tell me you're mine to command," he grumbled.

"Aren't I, sir?"

"Not with all the implications that phrase has," he muttered. "Let's not worry about that tonight. Come on, I fancy some fun."

He whispered an instruction to the nearest page, who ran off on swift feet. Their dance was relatively sedate, but they didn't leave the room afterwards and Ira wondered why until the next three dances had been played at double their normal speed. She saw the grin on Adeone's face.

"Sir?"

"They shouldn't gossip about me."

"I don't believe they all did, Your Highness."

"No, maybe not." He caught the eye of the conductor and winked. The dance slowed to its normal pace. Even the musicians looked relieved.

"Thank you, sir," said Ira carefully.

"Your evening, my lady."

Not knowing how to reply, she didn't. After a few minutes, they left for the Court Supper and she managed to excuse herself before he could suggest she sat on the dais. She was sure he was about to. It was meant to be an honour but the thought terrified her.

In the coach on the way home, her father said, "How many dances did the Prince ask you for?"

"Three, father."

"It might have been prudent to refuse the third."

"How? You always told me that I shouldn't refuse the FitzAlcis."

He sighed. "That is a complication, I admit, but there were whispers. I think tomorrow we have a quiet evening at home."

"Thank heavens for that," she replied, genuinely glad. If Adeone's interest had given her that, it might have been worth it. She was enjoying Court but after the day's events, following the ride the day before, time to adjust would be pleasant.

Chapter 8
ADVICE
Alunadai, Week 25 – 1st Ralal, 1st Ralis 1193
Court

AN ALUNA MONTH LATER, the Mundimri dawned with the members of the Court barely asleep. The feasting for the change of season had been exceptionally long. Beyond that consideration, it was also Prince Scanlon's birthday and there would be celebrations and entertainments for most of the day, with the children of courtiers allowed to attend, which meant, as Leila had observed, that people watched what they said more.

Ira woke a half hour before noon. There'd be no chance of a ride. Courtiers were expected at the Palace an hour after noon for the whole day. The younger members would be expected to keep an eye on the children. It made it less imposing for them than if it had been their parents. Ira remembered the excitement of attending, often in a new dress. The days had been happening since Prince Adeone was seven, maybe two or three a year, and would happen until Prince Scanlon was fifteen for certain. That would be another six years. Whether the King would continue them without there being young members of the FitzAlcis was anyone's guess. Though, she supposed Peaga Rathgar did count as the King's family and he would be around seven when Prince Scanlon was fifteen. She grinned to herself as she dressed. She could imagine how excited Leila, Elidir and Finn were. Aelia was still too young to attend even though she'd turned six the day before. Ira considered herself in the mirror. The dress was typical for the Mundimri, cool colours tended to prevail and her dress was a pale blue with darker embroidery. Pale colours did tend to drain her face of colour but this wasn't too stark. She didn't look wan. It was wrong for the star stone though, so she found a necklace that had been her grandmother's, sapphire and diamond stars set in silver.

She had a light breakfast of toast and jam. There was no point filling up. The feast would likely be a good one. If not, she'd eaten enough the previous evening to keep her going for days. Well, maybe until tomorrow. She slipped on her silk-upper shoes, tapping their well-heeled soles on the tiles of the hallway. She stopped with a wry grin when her father appeared.

He chuckled. "Come on. You can dance later."

"I'm not sure I want to, father. I've done so much dancing recently."

"It's impolite to refuse when asked," he replied.

She frowned to herself. That wasn't quite what he'd told her on her birthday and the Prince had danced with her most nights since, though maybe only once. She supposed he'd danced with Nia more and had asked Cornelia for a dance on occasion. He wasn't singling her out.

They arrived at Court at the same time as the Rales. Ira hugged Cornelia and winked at Finn. He looked almost grown up in a formal tunic with blue banding to mark him as Lord Rale's heir. He couldn't be addressed as 'Lord Finn' until he was fifteen, but the King still expected formal wear.

They entered the FitzAlcis Chamber together. Ira considered how much nicer it was than entering with just her father. It felt less intimidating. She, Cornelia and Finn excused themselves to their parents and crossed to where Leila and Elidir were already talking with Festus and Nia. Had they all arrived together? With no older siblings, Leila and Elidir would have been better arriving with someone closer to their age than just their father. She, Festus and Nia had arrived together. It eased younger members of Court into the assembly.

Ifor and Faran soon joined them. The small group had grown and was drawing unintentional notice. Most of the groups dotted around Court had no more than four people. Theirs had nine.

Festus whispered something to Finn and received a glare in reply that had Festus laughing.

Ira's eyes narrowed. "Stop it."

"Stop what?" enquired Festus innocently.

"Whatever it was you said. I don't trust that laugh."

Festus laughed again. "Would you like a dance, cousin? I think Finn was just about to ask Leila."

Ira's lips twitched. "I'm perfectly fine, thank you. Maybe Cornelia would prefer—"

"You're both as bad as each other," said Cornelia calmly. "Festus, I'll remove you at least."

They left with Nia's eyes following them. "They'd be well matched."

Ira shrugged. "The Prince needs to marry first."

"It's only tradition," said Faran. "I'm sure Festus has a way around it."

Ira caught his eye, chuckling. "He might. Would you like a dance?"

"Shouldn't I be the one to ask you, Lady Ira?"

"My cousin has been a formative influence," she said, straight-faced.

As they left the group, Faran remarked, "His Highness mentioned you dance well."

Ira blushed. "I expect he says it about most of the ladies, my lord."

Taking her hand to lead her to the dancefloor, he whispered. "He doesn't."

As they finished the simple dance, they noticed a rather red Finn and a calm Leila had entered.

"Who do you think is responsible for that?" Ira asked Faran.

"Someone who doesn't know how to read people. They're friends, nothing more. Just like you and Festus."

"We're cousins."

"It doesn't preclude friendship, my lady."

They were once more in the FitzAlcis Chamber when Prince Adeone arrived with his younger brother. Prince Scanlon was wearing a self-satisfied smile and a silk tunic that had bands of scarlet and emerald. Adeone's formal wear was banded in the same manner. Sons and heirs of the King it said to anyone practised in deciphering the Court. They accepted the obeisances of that Court with smiles and nods before crossing to the group. Rather than collecting Festus with a look, Adeone stayed for a time, talking with them all. Scanlon had a few words with Elidir, but was mostly silent. Ira wondered at that. Why would a nine-year-old not want to talk with his companion?

After a time, Adeone turned to her. "Might I request a dance, Lady Ira?"

Scanlon glanced at her. "You're not as pretty as he said."

Adeone pursed his lips. "Please excuse us, my lady." He bent down to his brother's ear and hissed, "It might be your birthday, but you do not insult the ladies of the Court! Apologise."

Ira pretended not to have heard. They all did.

Scanlon glared at his brother. "I apologise, Lady Ira."

"Thank you, Your Highness. I hope you're having a pleasant birthday."

"I was," he muttered. With a sigh, he added, "It has not been unpleasant, Lady Ira. I hope you will excuse Elidir and myself if we leave you now."

She forced a smile. "As my Prince wishes."

"He's been a right little termagant today," muttered Adeone to Festus after his brother left. "I really am sorry, Lady Ira."

"It's of no concern, Your Highness," she replied, trying to keep the peace. "So, you've said I'm pretty?" she added mischievously and marvelled at herself for doing so. Was she really teasing him?

Adeone actually blushed. "I'm going to kill him."

Festus chuckled. "No, you're not. His Majesty would be upset with you. Weren't you asking my cousin for a dance a few moments ago?"

"That's how you keep me in my place, everyone. Lady Ira, will you do me the honour, before I'm as helpful to your cousin?"

"It would be a pleasure, sir."

As they left the group, she said, "I hope Your Highness isn't too warm."

"Are you laughing at me, Lady Ira?"

"Never that, sir. We're at Court."

He burst into spontaneous laughter. "We are. Tomorrow, I'll come and dine at Macarian House."

"What?" exclaimed Ira. "I mean…erm… that would be an honour, sir."

"Invite Festus, Nia and Cornelia as well, if you'd be so kind."

"Anything you wish, Your Highness."

As they left the dancefloor quarter of an hour later, they passed Prince Lachlan, who was watching them shrewdly.

Adeone hesitated. "Uncle."

Ira curtsied and couldn't quite work out if Prince Lachlan was evaluating her or whether his gaze was always so direct.

"Lady Ira, would you do *me* the honour of a dance?"

"It would be a pleasure, Your Highness."

As they made their way to the dancefloor, Lachlan said, "Is my nephew annoying you?"

"Not at all, sir."

"Prince Scanlon mentioned he thought Prince Adeone was making you uncomfortable. I'd hope you would tell me if that were the case."

"His Highness' company is an honour, sir. I assure Your Highness it has not been uncomfortable."

"I'm glad to hear it," replied Lachlan. "Princess Lilith spoke well of Your Ladyship. She's missing your company."

Ira smiled. "Her Elegance was kindness itself to me, sir. I hope one day I can return her hospitality to others."

"I'm sure you'll have a chance, my lady."

As they danced, Ira tried not to consider the conversation but it kept intruding. Had Prince Scanlon really tried to make things difficult for his older brother? If so, why? Because he'd been told off in public? Well, it wasn't the wisest thing but he had been rude, and Prince Adeone was entitled to correct him in a way others there couldn't. None of those present would have talked about it either, but Prince Scanlon didn't know them so well. Maybe he didn't appreciate being reprimanded in front of Elidir. It did rather detract from the perception of a prince in control of his own life and everything around him.

When the dance finished, Prince Lachlan said, "May I escort you to your friends, Lady Ira?"

She smiled. "I wouldn't be a bother, sir. I don't know where they'll have hidden themselves this time."

He chuckled. "Then we shall enjoy the hunt together. Your father would never forgive me if I let you wander through Court alone. I'm sorry we've not spoken before tonight."

"Your Highness has far more calls on your time. The dance was an honour unlooked for."

"And in that, you do yourself a disservice, my lady." He drew her to a quiet part of the room. "Princess Lilith spoke of Your Ladyship as someone who needs no instruction in the ways of Court. I think she was right, but if I might counsel you, learn to be yourself here as well. You've grown into a remarkable young lady. Festus can be too boisterous; I know you're close, but be careful."

"Thank you. I will, sir."

"What would you say if it wasn't me?" he asked wryly.

Ira chuckled. "Probably, 'you can say that again' about my cousin, sir."

He laughed. "I like young Festus. He's been a good friend to Adeone. I hope it continues. Whatever their fathers think." He stopped himself. "You do listen well. Lilith was right about that. I imagine people are queuing up to tell you their secrets."

"I have heard a few, sir. Mostly they tell me other people's."

"Oh dear. Shall we continue?"

She nodded. They passed through the Lufian Room where Prince Scanlon, the Lux, Terans, Rathgars, Anguis and Para children were all clustered together. Ira pretended not to see the suspicious, then supercilious look on Prince Scanlon's face. Would Prince Lachlan later reprimand him?

He courteously left her with Cornelia and Faran in the FitzAlcis Chamber before returning the way they'd come. Ira watched him. There were a myriad of connections between the rooms of Court, so very few people retraced their steps. Faran had noticed.

"What caught his interest, Lady Ira?"

"I couldn't say, my lord."

Cornelia watched her. "Did you dance with His Highness?"

Ira swallowed. "He asked me to. I couldn't refuse."

"And Prince Adeone?" enquired Faran.

"Yes." She saw their faces. "What? We know Prince Adeone isn't going to marry me. Where's Nia?"

"Dancing," said Cornelia. "With Ifor," she added pointedly.

Ira sighed. "That reminds me, Prince Adeone has invited himself to dinner at Macarian House tomorrow. He wants you, Nia and Festus there."

"Why?"

"I might have said I couldn't tease at him at Court."

Faran burst out laughing. "He'd have liked that. Just accept his friendship, Ira. You've a similar sense of humour beneath your ladylike reserve."

She sighed. "I don't think I could let my guard down. There's too much at stake. They could ignore the inheritance laws."

"Not if you're his friend though," said Cornelia quietly. "He's more likely to ignore them if you refuse the hand of friendship for propriety."

"I can't win, can I?" murmured Ira despondently. "Everyone wants me to be something different. It's only—" she stopped. She'd been going to say it was only Lex who saw her as herself.

"Go and play elsewhere, Lord Faran."

The Lord of Lufian crooked an eyebrow. "Of course, Lady Cornelia. It's obviously exactly what my conscience demanded."

Once he'd gone, Cornelia said, "Stop trying to be what everyone wants. Start being who you want to be."

"That's what Prince Lachlan effectively told me, but I can't, can I? Father—"

"Times change. You've two of the FitzAlcis telling you they want to see who *you* are, not see the courtier. You're a far more refined courtier than I am, but you don't have to be that away from here."

"I…" She cursed quietly. "I don't know who I am under all this."

"We do," said Cornelia. "You're kind, caring, honest, enjoy teasing your friends and are a true lady."

"Someone could similarly describe you."

"But we're not talking about me, so stop changing the subject."

"I prefer the new subject," remarked Ira.

Cornelia chuckled. "Come on, let's go for a walk in the gardens."

When her father heard they would be entertaining Prince Adeone the following evening, he had less to say than Ira expected. There'd be panic when he told his staff, but they had, on a rare occasion, entertained King Altarius, Prince Lachlan and Lady Amara. In comparison, Prince Adeone should be far simpler.

Chapter 9
DINNER

THE EVENING CAME with unnatural alacrity. Ira wondered what to wear, but mindful of the advice of the previous evening, she picked her purple dress. If the Prince was after friendship, he wouldn't want to see her in formal attire. Her father's eyes narrowed but that was as much comment as he made.

Prince Adeone entered their house, removing his cloak and passing it to his manservant. Ira hesitated. Did he always bring his own attendant? Maybe he did. Festus had mentioned the man on several occasions.

"Have I beaten Lord Festus?"

"You have. It does him good, sir," said Ira quietly.

Her father stilled beside her.

"Welcome to our home once again, Your Highness," said Macaria. "I apologise if my daughter gave offence."

"Absolutely no offence whatsoever," replied Adeone airily. "Maybe when Her Ladyship has other company, we could talk over a couple of minor matters before we settle in to the evening."

"Of course, Your Highness."

Ira smiled. "I can look after myself, sir. More than used to it."

Adeone watched her appraisingly. "In which case, Macaria, we shall retreat to your study."

When they'd gone, she bit her lip. Her father wouldn't be happy, but the Prince didn't seem to mind. She wondered what their conversation would be. Would her father be apologising for her again?

By the time Prince Adeone entered the drawing room, Festus, Nia and Cornelia had all arrived. They all rose as the Prince entered. Ira didn't miss the glance between her cousin and guest. Something in that look made her consider if Festus had been purposefully late.

Half an hour of innocuous chatter later, Adeone said, "It's a shame it's dark. I would have loved to explore your gardens, Lady Ira."

Before she could reply, Festus said, "Take a walk anyway, sir. The moons are bright."

"True. Will you accompany me?"

Ira started. He was talking to her. "Of course, if you wish it, sir."

The prince's manservant passed them their cloaks. Had it been planned?

Adeone took his. "Thank you. I won't need anything else until we're at dinner, Simkins."

As they left for the gardens, Ira noticed Nia's face. There was the shadow of something she couldn't name. It wasn't jealousy but it was appraising.

They took the same path as she, Cornelia and Leila had. They were in full view of the house, and Ira felt safer because of it.

"I'm truly sorry for what my brother said last night, Ira."

She drew a sharp breath. His informality was disorientating. "He's young, Your Highness. We've all said things we shouldn't when we're young."

"Not Highness, please. Let me be just Adeone."

She studied his face briefly. The moonlight etched its line into sharp relief. "What do you want of me, sir?"

He stared ahead. "Friendship, laughter... You mean a lot to Festus, to Cornelia, even to Faran. Cousin Tyler has nothing but good to say of you, and yet you keep me at arm's length."

She hesitated. "You looked through me for years!"

"No, I just didn't look at you," he said. "For which incivility I humbly and sincerely apologise. I was too wrapped up in who I had to be. Well, I was too wrapped up in fighting who I had to be." He smiled wryly. "Father's sending me to do the Bayan Provincial Review in spring. I can't escape it any longer. I'm to bring Cousin Tyler back with me. He's staying here. I've just been discussing it with your father."

Ira swallowed. "It will be nice to return Her Elegance's hospitality."

"Yes," said Adeone. "I expect it will, but do you mind?"

She considered how to answer. He was being far softer than she'd ever known him to be. There was no edge of mischief about him and she realised she didn't miss it.

"It really will be a pleasure. I like Tyler. He's also kind."

"I don't know him. Oh, we've written but we've never met. I've too many people like that. It's expected we'll keep in contact but... they don't know me. They think they do. Festus thinks he does."

"Doesn't he? He's your closest confidant."

Adeone hesitated. "Yes, but... He hasn't the responsibility I have. We laugh and joke, and I'd be lost without him, but he doesn't see my soul."

"I don't think anyone ever truly sees the soul of another. Watch your step here. The stones are loose."

Adeone held out his arm. "Then let me steady you."

She chuckled. "Are you this chivalrous to Nia and Cornelia?"

"When they let me be. Nia hears too many of Festus' stories."

"She loves you very much."

"Yes," said Adeone with an odd inflection. "Cornelia, on the other hand, just organises us."

"She's an older sister," replied Ira, amused. "She's good at keeping people in order. Always has been." She shivered. The winter chill was descending.

Adeone took off his cloak. "Use this. It's far thicker than yours."

"Won't you be cold?"

"It'll do me good. I have to get out of this maudlin mood. Uncle Lachlan said you listened well and knew everyone's secrets because of it."

She giggled. "I never found out his." Was Adeone really making her laugh so easily?

"He hinted the opposite. So what has your cook decided to serve me?"

"Humble pie, obviously."

His eyes narrowed. "Are you teasing me?"

"Yes. I think he decided that stew and dumplings might go down well. He mentioned something about pudding being a surprise."

"He's definitely Marnin's brother," muttered Adeone. "I get worried when things are going to *be a surprise* with that family. Though I will say, there's not often I get a good stew."

"Then I hope it's a good one, otherwise someone else will be in a stew."

"You're incorrigible, Ira."

She smiled sweetly. "I'm a true lady of the Court."

He snorted. "You are, *at Court*."

"You were the one who invited yourself to dinner. Don't blame me."

He drew her into the shadows under an oak tree. "I am." He moved her hair off her face. "I wish you'd tease me more." He took her hand. "Will you let me visit again before I go to Garth?"

"How can I refuse?" Her heart was beating harder than ever. Why had he wanted to take this walk away from her cousins?

"No is an easy word."

"It's the most difficult one there is." She'd replied unthinkingly.

"Practise on others," he whispered. "Let me visit for quiet evenings."

She blinked. She couldn't say no, and she wasn't sure she wanted to. "As long as I can be myself, Adeone."

He kissed her fingers. "So I would hope. Let us dine."

Ira flushed immediately on re-entering the drawing room. The warmth after the cool of the gardens brought colour to her face.

"Been up to anything we should know about, Ira?" enquired Festus.

"No! We took a walk."

"Sounds too defensive to me."

Cornelia tossed a cushion at him. "Shut up. You shouldn't be let out."

"I have to agree," said Adeone, sitting down. "Bed without supper?"

"Your Highness is too kind," replied Festus with a grin. "Or at least, I hope you are. I hate going against my Prince."

"Doesn't mean you wouldn't," replied Adeone.

Divested of cloaks, Ira sat next to Nia and squeezed her hand. Her cousin glanced at her with that unfathomable expression, but before Ira could say anything, her father entered to say dinner was ready.

As they took their places, Ira frowned at the stew. It was as though Abe had known they needed a dinner that wouldn't spoil. Had he really talked to his brother and knew the Prince's tastes? Or was it more than that? She had a stern word with herself. She'd be seeing ghosts next, if she questioned every eventuality.

The stew, served with herby dumplings and crisp bread, was soon gone. Apparently, Prince Adeone did enjoy the hearty simplicity of it. Simkins removed his plate and refilled it without a word said. So the manservant could either read small telltale signs or knew the Prince exceptionally well. Festus looked at Simkins with what Ira called his pleading face. The manservant laughed.

"Pass me your plate, Lord Festus."

Seeing Ira's grin, Adeone said, "We're still growing."

"Outwards," muttered Festus to peals of laughter.

"Festus Landis—" started Lord Macaria, but stopped at a glance from Simkins.

Did the Prince's manservant really control what people would say in Adeone's presence? Ira puzzled over that, wiping up the last of the gravy on her plate. She supposed it stopped the Prince having to comment, but the complexities of roles perplexed her. Everything was far more intricate than it appeared. Were there double and hidden meanings in everything they all did?

A bowl of lemon meringue appearing in front of her distracted her thoughts. She glanced at her father, who was frowning slightly, then at the Prince who simply winked. She wondered just who had been giving orders and how much warning Abe had actually had. Slow-cooked stew and meringue took hours to prepare, even a day, and yet Abe hadn't, apparently, known until that morning that the Prince was expected. He could have prepared the stew anyway, but the meringue, no. Someone had known the Prince was going to invite himself before last night.

When Adeone and her friends had left, she put the question to her father. Who had known? He hesitated.

"Prince Adeone told me he'd be dining here during the Mundimri feast two nights ago. I shouldn't have pretended otherwise."

"Why did you?"

"He asked me to keep it private. I think he didn't want the Court to find out. I think young Festus knew also, though I didn't expect him to be late."

Ira hesitated. "I rather suspect he intended to be late, father."

"What did you discuss with His Highness?"

"He asked for my informal friendship."

Her father crooked an expressive eyebrow.

"Not that sort of informal friendship. Just a request that I don't act the courtier here. I think he's lonely," the words left her involuntarily.

"I expect he's many things. Go to bed, little Ira. It's been a long day."

As she dropped to sleep, Ira thought of the shadows under the tree and Adeone's hand in hers. It didn't warm her in the way the memory of Wynfeld's strength and laughter had. She'd take a ride in the morning.

Chapter 10
GUARDS

WYNFELD HELPED HER MOUNT the following morning without saying a word. They rode out towards the Wynwood again and, once clear of the city, he drew level with her.

"So, Jack reckons you're not riding as much because I did something I shouldn't."

Ira sighed. "No, you did everything you should, but I… just fancied a bit of time to myself."

"An aluna-month?"

She blushed. "I'm sorry, Lex. I had to sort a few things out and Court has drained me," she lied far too easily.

He snorted. "You've been busy all right. Was it for you Prince Adeone visited last night?"

"He had things to talk over with father."

"That's not quite the impression we all had."

She looked at him. "I don't think it's like that. He's not after me. He'll be marrying Nia."

"Has there been an announcement?"

Ira blushed. "No. As far as I know, he's not asked her yet, but it's been obvious for years."

"That they're like brother and sister, yes," said Wynfeld, gazing ahead. "I hate to say this, my lady, but His Highness is riding towards us and not looking through you."

Ira cursed under her breath. "Thank you for stating the obvious. You should give lessons in it."

"I did, my lady, to you."

Ira struggled to keep a straight face as Adeone drew level and manoeuvred his horse into step, Ira moving forward slightly so he could.

"Morning, Lady Ira."

"Good morning, sir. I hope you've had a pleasant ride."

"I have, but don't wish to return yet. Do you mind if I accompany you?"

"Erm, I don't wish to refuse Your Highness but what of the rumours?"

He sighed. "I don't give two hoots of a deaf owl, but I accept the point." He turned to the two guards with him. "Jenner, stay and see Her Ladyship is safe."

Ira swallowed. "I do have an escort, sir."

Adeone's gaze raked over Wynfeld. "So I see. Jenner will stay with you anyway."

"Thank you, sir." Ira watched him ride off, cursing to herself. She had never needed a guard and didn't particularly want his spy with her.

The guard sensed her unease. "It's all right, my lady. I know not to see or hear anything. Been guarding the Prince for a couple of years. He doesn't always appreciate our presence."

"Thank you, but I'm only out for a ride, not secret assignations."

"Never thought differently, my lady."

'No,' thought Ira, *'because I'm too much of lady to be having them.'*

By the time the guard left her at Macarian House, she'd had no chance to continue her conversation with Wynfeld. She saw to her morning duties and then wandered to the stables. Jack eyed her.

"He's not here."

She sighed. "Where?"

"Sent him on a few errands that will take him a while."

"On purpose?" asked Ira shrewdly.

Jack's lips twitched. "What was with your guard earlier, m'lady?"

"We bumped into Prince Adeone and His Highness insisted. I could hardly refuse. I'll be riding again tomorrow." She saw Jack's face. "And will expect Wynfeld to accompany me."

He chuckled. "Never doubted it, m'lady."

* * *

A week later, Ira said, "I'd almost think you're planning this, Your Highness."

His lips twitched. "Your routine is rather predictable, Lady Ira, and I'm reliably informed I used to look right through you."

"I'm equally informed, Your Highness, that you never looked at me."

They both laughed.

Ira bit her lip. "However, sir, the Court is already whispering about our dances. If someone spots these morning talks, and the fact you are lending me a guard—"

He waved everyone out of hearing, waiting until they were. "Lady Ira, there are always discontented souls and I do not want to lose you to one."

"So you offer this protection to Festus, Nia and Cornelia?"

"Sometimes," he admitted. "They have much to say on the matter too."

"Good. Do you not think by ensuring I have a guard, you are drawing attention to a target?"

"I—" He cursed. "You're right. I'll take them away with me. I'm already a target."

"You're not, sir."

He sighed. "Bayans may feel differently."

"Not if Her Elegance has anything to do with it. Anyway, your father executed the traitors and beggared the rebels. I don't think you need to worry overmuch. Princess Lilith hasn't been assassinated."

"True. I'll leave you to your ride."

"Thank you, sir."

Once they were alone, Wynfeld said, "How did you manage that?"

"With a dose of your honesty.

* * *

The following week, they were riding through the Wynwood when Ira reined in. The frost laden undergrowth captivated her. Its tendril crystals were catching the dappled light. She turned to Wynfeld, her eyes alight.

"I wish I could paint this."

He held her gaze. "I wish I could paint you."

Her heart beat faster as she held his gaze. "Help me dismount."

As he took her waist, the cold revealed her quick breaths. Wynfeld's hands were supportive as she landed on the woodland floor.

"Hold me."

He let go. "We should—"

"Lex." She took his hand. "Tell me you don't feel something."

"Doesn't matter what I feel or don't feel, my lady. I'm your groom."

She cursed. "You're more than that!"

"Am I? Can you honestly say that any of your friends know my name?"

"No, but I didn't want... I didn't want you hurt!"

He blinked. "Hurt?"

"They're... They don't understand what it's like to grow up without siblings. They'd never have understood our friendship."

"Is that what it is? Now?"

She hesitated. "Yes."

"What just happened—"

"Was a mistake."

"Like the last *mistake*. Well, we better not make it a habit. Not if the Prince is as interested as he seems."

Ira cursed. "I don't want him!"

"Do you think it's up to you?"

"Yes. They can't force me to say the words."

He scoffed. "Oh, they can, Ira. They can force us all."

She took his hand and held it fast. "You're who I want in my life, Lex! I know it now more than I ever knew it before. The Prince won't be here for a while. He's going to Garth. Just hold me!"

He worked his fingers through hers. "I daren't. I don't know where it'll end, Ira."

"I won't let you go too far, Lex," she whispered. "I won't."

He reached for her and she stepped into his embrace, sobbing. Every pent up emotion since her return from Garth flowed out of her without a thought. He wrapped his cloak around her and the warmth held her fast. His breathing calmed. Maybe this was what they had needed to dispel the thought of anything else.

"Ira…"

She ignored the whisper. She didn't want to hear whatever he wanted to say. She was being reckless, but if anyone found them, she'd say she'd taken a fall.

"Ira…"

The whisper was more insistent. She glanced up. He motioned with his eyes. There, in the dappled light of winter, stood a white stag, its antlers almost too heavy for its head. She smiled, watching it watching them before it bounded away.

"They're meant to be lucky," whispered Wynfeld.

"It's just its winter coat."

"I'll take the luck. We should be getting home."

She nodded. "Thank you."

* * *

A week later Ira had spent seven consecutive mornings riding with Wynfeld, enjoying his company and teasing. She was wondering if she could somehow persuade Maria into letting them have a stolen evening of talk and games, as they used to, when Leo announced Prince Adeone. Ira hastily rose and nodded for Leo to wait.

"Father's at Court, sir."

"Oh. I should have checked. Would you like your maid to be present?"

Ira considered. The correct thing was to say 'yes' but she didn't. "I'm sure no-one would question Your Highness' honour. Leo, could you bring us some tea, please?" Watching the footman leave with a slight bow to Adeone, Ira waved her guest to a seat. "I hope you don't mind tea, sir."

Adeone snorted. "It is an effective way of stopping a lot of rumours, Ira." He sank into the chair. "Maybe we should ask for cake or biscuits when they bring our drinks."

Her lips twitched. "I'm sorry if I've presumed, sir."

"Quite the opposite." He studied her for a moment. "I thought we'd gone beyond the courtier here. Please do sit down."

"Oh, sorry." Ira took her place with a slight blush. Seeing Adeone's crooked eyebrow made her flush deepen.

He chuckled. "I do hope it's only me that has this effect on you."

She rubbed at her neck. "You are known to excel at all you do."

"If only that were true," he muttered. "Advisor Gillham has been putting me through my paces today and I can't say it's gone well."

"Gillham?" asked Ira, confused.

"My tutor. Oh, yes, I'm still under a tutor. When I leave for Garth it ends, but until then I have to suffer."

How to reply? She couldn't show pity. "How long until you leave?"

"Second week of spring. Are you trying to get rid of me?"

"Not at all, sir… Adeone. Would you like anyone else to join us this evening?"

"Definitely not. Festus has to study. Spending time alone with Nia and Cornelia is as dangerous as being on our own here, but at least I'm wrecking all your reputations equally."

Unsure whether to be amused or not, Ira said, "I've always heard you're even handed."

He sighed. "Why is everything turned positive around me?"

"It could be your father's influence. I hear he has a bit."

Adeone chuckled. "Yes. I thought you'd agreed not to be a courtier though. So, why are you being one?"

They exchanged a long look. Ira flushed again. Her face burned. She'd annoyed him when he was already feeling low. Why had he disturbed her quiet evening if he was unhappy? Friendship, she reminded herself, was for the low moments as well as the high.

"It's difficult not to be one after so much drilling by governesses."

"Let us walk in your gardens. I don't care that it's dark."

Ira hesitated. "And cold?"

"For two minutes."

She pushed herself to her feet and followed him. They walked down the steps onto the lawn. She took his hand out of politeness when he held it out to aid her descent, but he didn't let it go at the bottom.

She tried to release his hand but he tightened his grip. "Tell me about your gardens."

What did he want to know? She started with her earliest memories and moved on to helping Whyte choose plants and design flower beds. By the time they were halfway around the lawns, Adeone had relaxed. He let her hand go as though he'd only just realised he was holding it. They finished their walk still talking about plants. On re-entering the drawing room, Ira flushed once more, the warmth from the fire hitting her.

Adeone cursed himself for a fool. "I shouldn't… I should take my mood elsewhere."

She watched his face. "Not before you've had some tea and told me why your mood is so low."

"I don't want to inflict…"

"Bit late," observed Ira with twinkling eyes. "Here's your tea, there's a chair and I'm listening."

Adeone chuckled. "Oh, it's nothing. It's all this work for Garth. It's making me face my future and I, well, I'm realising I can't continue as I have been. No more *fun*."

"Why not? It's part of who you are."

"A King's Representative can't be a prankster."

"In the normal way of things, but you're also his son. Anyway," her eyes brightened, "blame Festus."

"Now there's an idea." His lips twitched. "You'd have me destroy the reputation of a future Lord of Oedran?"

"I'm sure my cousin needs no help with that!"

He laughed openly, then sobered. "Do we have to grow up, Ira?"

"Yes, but we needn't grow wise. Everyone has been telling me to be myself. Yet there's Court, friend, cousin, mistress all wrapped up within me. Who am I? Do I have to be the same person at Court as to here in private, or when I'm talking with our steward? That's the dilemma we all have. Who are we? We are all our personas but do they all need to be the same? Are you the same person in private as when you're discussing the empire with advisors?"

Adeone held her gaze. "I don't have advisors yet."

"Then maybe this is the time to decide if you have to be the same person for all your different days."

His gaze never wavered. "I'm sorry."

"What for?"

"Not understanding it isn't easy to change how you act."

She shrugged. "You were right, though, weren't you? I was trying to be everything to everyone. No-one can keep that up."

He frowned. "You're right. I mustn't disturb your evening any further. I can see myself out."

Rather perplexed, she watched him go. Had she said something wrong? Was he annoyed at her presumption? He'd wanted her to be herself in private and they'd been in private. She put her head in her hands. Did she even care? It wasn't as though he'd taken much thought for her comfort, appearing without warning, insisting on a cold evening stroll through the rimed garden and then laughing at her. Yet there was something in his mood she recognised all too easily. Had he just needed space? Had he realised he shouldn't talk of his angst with her? Was it a compliment that he had? Too many questions.

When her father returned, she told him of Prince Adeone's visit. To her surprise, he already knew.

"I spoke with His Highness at Court. He was complimentary of your brief hospitality."

"He was here for a good half hour, father."

"That is brief. He also sent his apologies for abruptly leaving. He said he remembered His Majesty expected him to preside at Court."

Ira swallowed. Had he really recalled that? She couldn't but wonder if it was something else. There'd been an odd look in his eye as he frowned. She excused herself for the evening and made her way to her bedchamber.

Maria's eyes narrowed as she entered. "So, why was His Highness here?"

"He was thirsty," said Ira. "Can we get an evening of cards and games, Maria? You, me and Lex as we used to?"

Maria sighed. "You know why we can't, Ira. I'm sorry."

She slumped onto the bed. "Growing up shouldn't mean I have to lose my friends!"

"You've not lost me or Lex."

She swallowed. "Haven't I? Oh, I know you're right. Nia's being distant with me as well. I didn't ask for the Prince's attention. I don't even particularly want it. I don't mean that I dislike him. I just don't feel anything for him, particularly. I can act his friend, but it is an act."

"Is it?" asked Maria.

Ira went quiet. After several moments, she said, "Mostly an act."

Maria sat by her and gave her a one-armed hug. "All friendships start that way. Well, most. You have to be acquaintances before you are friends."

"What should I do?"

"Stop questioning everything. I know you do it. Let whatever friendship could be there develop. It'll become clear to both of you if it's not working."

"It might have done. He left abruptly. All right. I'll stop looking for reasons or thinking I did something wrong."

Maria chuckled. "I'll believe that when I see it."

* * *

Festus met her on her return from her morning ride. Lex took her mare to stable, as though he was nothing more than a groom, but that morning's embrace still burned within her. They were playing a risky game, but his support had laid to rest the ghosts of the previous evening.

"Don't tell me, Festus, you're inviting yourself to breakfast."

"Yes. I tried to persuade Nia to as well, but she thought it would be too much of an imposition. I'm not sure what's up with her at the moment. She's a little down."

Ira sighed. "Is it because Prince Adeone's widened his circle?"

"You mean is it because of you?" Festus shrugged. "It could be, but His Highness is still dining at Landis House and seeing her. I wouldn't have thought Nia would be jealous."

"I hope not because I'm not interested in the Prince like she is."

Festus chuckled. "It doesn't mean he's not interested in you."

She rounded on him. "Is he?"

"Keep your hair on. I don't know. I was just theorising." He grinned. "Apparently, he called by last night."

She glared at him. "He did and then left very abruptly." She paused. "You'd tell me, wouldn't you, Fes, if he was going to break Nia's heart?"

He hesitated. "Yes, but it doesn't mean he'd tell me."

Chapter 11
MUNLUMEN EVE

IRA READIED HERSELF for the Munlumen festivities of Court with more excitement than she normally felt. Winter's end was always her favourite time as bulbs sprouted and colour returned. Her dress was new, a much deeper colour than the one for the Mundimri, but still it didn't enhance the star stone. Should she wear another pendant? No. They had the stone. Why not show it off?

Winter had been an awkward time at Court. It seemed everyone had a view on the developing friendship between her and the Prince. He'd dine at Macarian House at least once a week, sometimes with others present, sometimes alone. He did the same with others: the Landises, Irises and Rales. Why was it so notable that he was doing it with them? Still, a friendship of sorts had developed, and he was courteous to her at Court without being overly attentive. She had noticed him watching her on several occasions but he watched many courtiers. It was part of Court life. She just wished he'd hurry up and ask Nia to marry him.

Court seemed no different. All her friends and cousins were there. They stood talking as normal, dancing as normal, laughing as normal. None of them expected Lord Ryson to approach them as presiding lord.

"Lady Ira, may I have a word?"

She moved aside with him. He'd never been someone whom she had warmed to, though he was never patronising or unwelcoming when she called on Leila and Elidir.

"Prince Adeone wonders if you'll do him the honour of sitting with him at the feast?"

Ira hesitated. "I would not like to draw such attention, my lord."

"And courtiers do not refuse the FitzAlcis. I shall tell him you would be honoured."

She gave a brief bob as he left. Flushing, she rejoined her friends. Faran looked at her kindly.

"Let's take a walk, Lady Ira."

They left for the gardens. She didn't want the eyes of the Court on her any sooner than they would be. He asked her what Lord Ryson had said and on hearing the reply murmured,

"Festus tried to talk Adeone out of it."

So they'd been discussing her. Her face muscles tightened involuntarily. Festus had assured her they hadn't.

"Lady Ira, Prince Adeone only mentioned it as a possibility. We didn't spend hours discussing you or anything like that. Festus said you'd feel uncomfortable and I mentioned there were other ways of showing favour if he wanted to. Apparently, we didn't dissuade him, which means he wants you there for a reason."

"I realise that. I just wish I knew what the reason was! His *favour* could damage me as much as it could help. Until he's married, all of this speculation isn't helping any of us."

"I will tell him you're concerned. No, my lady, please let me. Your angst troubles my conscience and I think you have many valid points. I can't now stand by and let him do this."

Ira sighed. "I... I just wish he'd ask Nia and be done with it."

When Adeone escorted her to her place at the dais, silence rippled amongst the courtiers, followed by conversations hastily resumed. They waited for the King to seat himself before they took their places and Adeone squeezed her hand under the table. She hardly ate anything from the selection of roast meats, rich gravies, pies, soups, crackers and cheese laid out in front of them. The Prince's server quietly asked if she'd prefer anything else, but it wasn't that she didn't like what was on offer, she just couldn't swallow. The entertainment that evening was a troupe of Bayan dancers and acrobats. As she watched them twirl, Adeone whispered,

"The Exarch trying to gain favour before my visit."

She chuckled. "I am sure he wouldn't stoop to such tactics, Your Highness. Are you looking forward to your visit?"

"I am. It should be interesting to see Garth. I hear it's beautiful."

Talk turned to the wonders of the city and Ira managed to find a form of ease. She was highly aware of the eyes on them. When the entertainment ended, the King rose and took his leave of those seated closest. Two seats away, Ira merely smiled and curtsied as he wished her goodnight. Was she dreaming or did his gaze linger on her slightly longer than on others?

To her surprise, her father never mentioned her being seated with the Prince as they returned home. He'd collected her as the Prince retired for the evening and escorted her to their coach without saying a word. She supposed he couldn't know how well she'd deported herself from his seat further down the dais and wouldn't be told for hours. It didn't stop her being relieved. She wanted to understand the evening before answering for it.

* * *

The following morning, her father didn't appear for breakfast. Rather perplexed, she went to his study to find he wasn't there either. She knocked and entered the steward's office.

"Piers, do you know where His Lordship is?"

"At the Palace, my lady. The King required his presence."

"Do we know why?"

"I don't. I expect it's to do with the Macian Isles, my lady."

She nodded and left, no less perplexed. Her father had meetings with the King but the timing was curious. The first morning of any season was normally quieter.

She picked up her letters. A despatch rider had obviously arrived for there were several from Bayan. She crossed to the drawing room and started reading. She'd need to reply. Would it be wrong of her to ask Adeone to carry letters for her when he visited? He was leaving in a fortnight and it took a couple of weeks at cavalcade pace. Maybe she should just send her replies via the mail route.

Obviously, rumours of the Prince's favour had reached Bayan. Most of her friends there were asking about it. Princess Lilith, on the other hand, advised her to look at her own feelings. That was interesting. She'd had an arranged marriage.

Ira put the letters aside to reply to and went to check if there were any household matters requiring her attention. Discovering everyone was managing quite well without her, she requested her horse and went to Landis House. She found Nia in the drawing room looking underslept.

"You look shattered. What time did you get back?"

"We left not long after you," replied Nia. "I couldn't sleep."

"Why not?"

"Thoughts. Can you discourage the Prince?"

Ah. Ira had wondered when the subject would arise. "I have tried, Nia. Honestly, I've tried. He just wants my friendship. I can't refuse that, given who he is and the fact he's close to you and Festus. It would be really awkward for everyone if I did."

"But last night…"

"Last night was at Court. You know we can't refuse the FitzAlcis' requests there. I tried to but Lord Ryson wasn't going to let me. Lord Faran's said he'll ask Adeone not to put me in that position again. I want him to ask you. I don't understand why he hasn't."

"You're really not interested in him?"

"No! Anyway, I need to marry a second son. Someone who can help with the lordship when father's gone, who won't be distracted by their own concerns and who can give me sons to take on the lordship for our line. I really don't need to marry a prince! Nor do I want to."

Nia swallowed. "Has he given you any presents?"

"No. When he's called round of an evening, we've talked, mostly about Bayan and Garth. It's not surprising, is it? I lived there for almost a year and he's about to do the provincial review. If anything, I'd say he's utilising my knowledge rather than courting me."

Her cousin visibly relaxed. "I'm sorry."

Ira gave her a hug. "So am I. I didn't want any of this!"

Nia chuckled. "So what was sitting at the dais like?"

"Overwhelming. I felt sick throughout the whole thing and would happily have swapped. His Majesty's total addition to the conversation was to wish me goodnight. His Highness managed slightly more, but nothing extraordinary. I quite envied the rest of you."

Half an hour later, Festus' manservant entered. "Lady Ira, Lord Macaria has asked that you join him at home. Your horse is out front."

"Thank you, William." Once the manservant had left, she sighed. "He'll want his report on last night as well." She saw Nia's face. "He hardly spoke to me on the way home. We were both tired. Come to dinner soon."

Ira dismounted in the stableyard and noticed another horse there. She frowned slightly. "Jack, have we guests?"

"Aye, m'lady. Lord Iris arrived whilst His Lordship sent for you."

She nodded. That could mean a reprieve from her father's questions or something more sinister. Lord Iris was the King's Chief Advisor as well as her father's peer.

She knocked on her father's study door. Lord Iris or no Lord Iris, her father had sent for her, so there must be a reason.

"Ah, Ira. His Majesty and Prince Adeone will be joining us for dinner tomorrow, along with Lord Iris, Lord Faran and your cousins. Will you see to arrangements, please?"

"Of course, father. Lord Iris, will His Majesty have any preferences?"

"Beyond the fact His Highness has spoken highly of your cook, I do not believe so, Lady Ira. I think it would be wise to expect the King to wish to be private with your father and myself after the meal."

"Very good, my lord. Thank you."

As she left, silence followed her. What was happening? She went to Abe and gave him the good news.

"Don't you fret, Lady Ira. I'll manage it all."

Ira thanked him and turned to leave. She paused, eyeing a crate. "Abe, where are all these lemons coming from?"

He shrugged. "It's a good year for them, my lady."

"We never have this many!"

He looked shifty. "A new grocer, my lady."

"Via the Palace?" she enquired with narrowed eyes.

He blushed. "I believe they use the same supplier."

She left the kitchen, frowning. Nia's question about presents echoed. Adeone hadn't given her any presents, but this, this had to be his handiwork, in which case he had. Lemons weren't a cheap fruit, most came from Denshire and were reserved by the Palace. Why hadn't she noticed? She went on the hunt for Maria and found her in her own small sitting room.

"I don't know what to think."

Maria drew her down onto the small couch. "What's happened?"

Ira explained everything.

"I'd say it's pretty clear that His Highness is courting you."

"He wanted friendship! You told me friendship didn't matter."

"Nor did it, but you must see he wants more now."

Ira put her head in her hands. "I don't. I don't want more. I want him to marry Nia. She'd be far better than me for him."

"It's his choice, Ira."

"Do I have no say?"

Maria shrugged. "You might, if he asks you, but don't act in haste if he does."

"I need a ride."

"No, you need to tell me to see that the house is sparkling and arrange for the sheets to be changed on every bed in the morning, in case our guests need to stay the night. If they do, the King must have your father's chambers, so they need preparing in case."

Ira sighed. "Fine. I'll go and pretend I'm calm and collected about entertaining the King, Prince, Lord Iris and Lord Faran. My cousins I can just about cope with."

Maria chuckled. "Is Lord Faran so formidable?"

"No, he's a softy but he is a Lord of Lufian in his own right, and the King's ward. Do you think this meal is a test?"

Maria held her gaze. "Everything is a test, Ira Macaria."

* * *

The following evening, the King arrived with Prince Adeone and Lord Faran after Lord Iris and her cousins did, so they were all present to greet King Altarius. Ira tried hard not to judge his sweeping glance. He'd visited several times over the years, but she'd been much younger. Had he purposefully not visited since she was fifteen? It struck her that her father had virtually stopped entertaining his peers and the FitzAlcis since her fifteenth birthday, as though doing so when she was unmarried would have raised conjectures, which was ironic, seeing how the Prince had taken it upon himself to ignore the courtesy.

Ira was all too aware that, although they were an even number for dinner, the generational split was uneven. Should she have invited Lord Landis as well? No, she'd been given the guest list. Everyone there obviously had a purpose. Festus and Faran to keep Adeone company, Nia to keep her company. Hopefully, it wouldn't be a long evening, but the King would be the one to determine that.

Abe had decided on roast beef for the main course. The King seemed to appreciate it. Dessert he waved away, then saw it was a spiced fruit pudding and changed his mind.

"Have you pinched my undercook at Ceardlann, Macaria?"

"No, Sire. I employed his older brother."

Altarius laughed. "Ah. That would explain it. Lady Ira, please thank Abraham for me."

"Of course, Sire. Is there anything else Your Majesty would like?"

"A mellow whiskey, a pleasant fire and a quiet evening."

"I've asked them to see the library is provided with the promise of that at least, sir."

"Thank you, my lady. Maybe you'd join me, Macaria, Iris."

Everyone rose as the King did. Ira watched him, her father and Lord Iris leave. Adeone let out a long breath.

"What about us, Ira?"

"I thought drawing room and cards, sir."

"Sounds good. Nia, will you lend me your luck?"

Seeing the way her cousin's face lit up, Ira cursed Adeone's easy manner. It wasn't fair to toy with her cousin's affections if he wasn't courting her but maybe he was and using herself as cover. Ira cursed. Why did Court intrigue have so many facets?

Once in the drawing room, Simkins and Leo passed around drinks. Ira let the other four play cards. She wasn't bothered about joining in. Around two hours later, she left the drawing room and found the FitzAlcis menservants talking quietly.

"Does His Majesty require anything, Master Quinn?"

"No, my lady. Thank you. He's quite content. I'm not sure how long he'll be though."

"It's no concern. I just wished to make sure all was well."

Three hours later, her cousins, Faran and Adeone were talking quietly. Festus and Adeone exchanged puzzled glances. What was taking the King so long? Ira suspected Adeone knew very well. Festus was, if not pretending, attempting not to worry her into thinking there was a conspiracy. Once she suspected there was more to the lateness of the evening, she saw something else in their glances. Festus knew exactly what was happening and was remonstrating with Adeone.

She left the room. They could have their debate without her watching. The King's manservant smiled as she caught his eye.

"Will His Majesty be staying the night, Quinn?"

"I expect so, my lady. A quantity of whiskey has been consumed."

"Do we know when they're likely to retire?"

"I expect soon, my lady."

Ira re-entered the drawing room. "Quinn thinks His Majesty will stay the night. Does anyone else wish to?"

Festus shook his head. "Nia and I will go home. It's not far."

Adeone smiled. "You get Nia home, Festus. I'll explain to father."

"Can we go via the Palace and drop anyone there?"

Faran snorted. "It's completely the wrong direction. Go home, Festus! Nia's already half asleep." He passed Ira a drink with a smile.

Once her cousins had left. Ira curled into a chair. "What about you two?"

"See, Faran, I told you that she'd learn to cope with being informal."

Faran ignored the Prince. "Do you have room for us, my lady?"

"Of course. We're a small family."

He laughed. "It's still a family."

"I'm sorry…" she'd momentarily forgotten he was an only child and an orphan.

He kissed her fingers. Acknowledgement that she didn't need to apologise or acceptance of her apology, she wasn't sure. She listened as he and Adeone began a quiet conversation. She started awake when Faran knelt by her.

"Go to bed, Lady Ira. We can look after ourselves."

"His Majesty…"

"I'll explain to father," said Adeone. "We've kept you up for too long."

She blinked sleepily at him. "I'll be fine."

"Nonsense." He hesitated, then motioned Faran aside. Lightly as though she weighed less than a sword, he picked her up. "Where's your room?"

She tried to object, but his arms were comfortable, and she rested her head on his shoulder. She mumbled instructions and half fell asleep against him.

He gently laid her on her bed and undid her bodice, but didn't remove it. Her breathing deepened, and she felt the blanket drape over her shoulders.

On the edge of consciousness, she heard him leave and thought he said, "That's not helped," but her dreams claimed her.

* * *

She awoke the following morning embarrassed and uncomfortable. Had the Prince really carried her to bed? She couldn't believe it, but her body told her it was true. She had to get up and dress and see to breakfast. If the King had stayed, then would he breakfast here or at the Palace?

She entered the dining room to find King Altarius and her father both present. The King pushed himself to his feet.

"My apologies for last night, my lady. I didn't realise how late we were talking. I hope it didn't inconvenience you."

"Not at all, Sire. I hope you had a restful night."

"Very, my lady, but I shouldn't disturb your morning any further. I believe my coach should be waiting. Macaria, I hope to see you soon."

They both walked with the King to see him safely off.

As they closed the front door, Ira said, "Prince Adeone and Lord Faran?"

"Went home last night. It disappointed me that you went to bed."

Ira swallowed. "Prince Adeone carried me to bed, father. I didn't have much choice in the matter."

"Come to my study when you've had breakfast."

Ira nodded and left for the dining room. The summons didn't help her appetite or her digestion.

Macaria watched her enter and waited for the door to close. "Your hospitality impressed the King last night, Ira. I'm proud of the way you coped. I hope you are as well."

"I shouldn't have fallen to sleep, father."

"That was unfortunate, but not unexpected. Why did His Highness carry you to bed?"

"You'd have to ask him. I was half asleep."

"Ira!"

She sighed. "It's true. Faran woke me, telling me to go to bed, but Adeone waved him aside and picked me up. He didn't let me object."

"I will discuss it with His Highness then, should opportunity present itself. The only people he should carry to bed are his wife, children and mistresses. I would hope you're not the last."

She blushed. "I'm certainly not!"

"Good. We're expected at Court this evening."

Chapter 12
PROPOSAL

THE DAY BEFORE ADEONE departed for Garth, Ira was writing in her journal when Leo announced him. She smiled distractedly before noticing something in his eyes that said she needed to lose her preoccupation. She put her pen aside. The machinations of the Court the previous evening could easily wait.

"Would you like refreshments, sir?"

"Not for me, thank you, Lady Ira. I would like not to be disturbed."

She nodded at Leo, who left with a definite emphasis. Ira's skin tingled as she watched Adeone. There was a presence to him that hadn't been there before. As though he had remembered he was a prince, or, more accurately, a man with a future to fit. He crossed to the window, examining the view. Still on her feet, she waited. He must have much on his mind before his departure.

"Can we walk, Lady Ira?"

"Of course, sir."

He knew the paths well enough now and she was only slightly perplexed when he took one to lead them out of sight of the house. Still, she'd spent hours alone with him, so thoughts of propriety seemed pointless. She followed his steps and his silence.

He paused under the apple tree, chuckling. "Did you really climb this?"

"Yes, sir. It was a moment of aberration." She put her hand on the trunk, looking up at the branch where she'd sat.

"It's certainly not the lady you are now."

"No, it's not. Can I help with whatever troubles you?"

"It's why I'm here," he admitted turning to her. He took her hand, kissing her fingers, turning it over, he kissed her palm. "Lady Ira Macaria, I would like to marry you, for you to marry me. No, hush. Don't give me your answer immediately." His fingers tightened their grip. "Think about it, please. Tell me when I return from Garth."

He brushed her hair off her face again. Gentle as the breeze in spring. His eyes were soft, alluring and pools of calm. She didn't know how to react. He stepped forward. She tried to step back but the tree was behind her. She closed her eyes. He was going to kiss her, but the kiss never came. She blinked. Adeone was watching her.

"You don't feel the same."

Her heart raced. "I thought you loved Nia. That there was no hope—"

"I did once." He sighed. "I find myself craving your company in a way I've never done with her. Dancing with you, I forget everyone else. Carrying you to bed, that… that was a mistake. I could have watched you sleep without a second thought, but that would have been so wrong of me. I want you in my life at my waking and retiring. Can you understand?"

She could but she *didn't* feel the same for him and he had realised. "I can, but it's come as something of a surprise, sir."

"Sir won't help," he observed wryly. "Father advised me to wait until I'd been to Garth—"

"Why?"

"I don't know. I wanted to give you time though, as I thought it only fair. Let me leave for Garth on a promise that you'll consider it."

She nodded. "I shall consider it, Adeone."

"Thank you. Will you be at Court?"

"I hadn't planned to be," she lied. There was no way she was going to Court after this.

He kissed her fingers again. "Then I will take my leave of you here. Whatever you decide, Ira, know you hold my heart."

'As if that's going to help!' she thought as she watched him leave without a backward glance. Drawing a deep breath, she left by a different path and slipped into the house by a side door. She ran up to her room wanting privacy. Why had he asked her? And why did he have to do it under the apple tree, of all places? Memories of laughing with Lex did not mix with such a serious proposal. Twelve minutes later, her maid informed her that her father wanted a word.

* * *

She entered the study, once more feeling like a naughty child. The appraising look her father gave her clearly said that he knew why Adeone had visited and wanted to know what her response had been; however he played his part well.

"Was His Highness well?"

"Yes, father." There was no point dragging out the ordeal. "He's proposed and asked that I consider my answer carefully."

He frowned. "You should have accepted immediately."

"How could I, sir? I need your advice." For once she was glad to use propriety against him.

"Are you so blind, Ira? Do you think I and the King would have allowed His Highness' visits and attentions if we didn't approve?"

"He was meant to ask Nia!" cried Ira.

"The King would never allow it. There's no way Prince Adeone can marry a Landis." He must have seen her confusion. "You don't need to know why. Lady Feronia's father should have put a stop to her hopes and dreams years ago. He's failed her by not doing so. You on the other hand do not present the same impediment."

"No, but it destroys our line."

"You'll birth a king. That is some legacy. Lord Iris and I have discussed the matter. Your third son, or the first son of your second son, will inherit the title."

"You've—" started Ira, outraged. "How long have you been planning this? Making a mockery of me?"

"No-one but I, Iris and the FitzAlcis have known about our negotiations. It was clear soon after your return that the Prince was interested. I'm disappointed it took you so long to realise."

"He was meant to ask Nia," she said again. "We all thought he'd ask Nia. Father, what do I say to her?"

"Will you marry Prince Adeone? Before you say anything to her, you need to make that decision. I will say, the King and I will be disappointed in you if you don't."

"Great," Ira snapped. "There's no pressure there, is there, father? I'm not deciding today and I'm *not* going to Court."

"If I insist?"

"Please don't," she replied, not wanting to make any threats she might regret having to keep.

"Very well. Tomorrow, however, we go."

* * *

The following morning, her ride with Wynfeld was far more sedate. She kept her saddle for the entire ride and hardly exchanged a word with him. She didn't want to marry Adeone, deal with the Court as a member of the FitzAlcis. She'd be the highest ranking lady there in the absence of a queen. The thought terrified her.

Unsurprisingly, Lex asked her if she was all right. Knowing she could tell him the truth, she said simply she wasn't feeling well. It was the truth. Her stomach roiled at the situation.

Festus was waiting for her again. Would she see more of him with the Prince away? Though she doubted that was why he'd invited himself to breakfast. Her father's cutting observation about interesting timing told her he didn't think it was a coincidence, either.

Once on their own, she said, "You know?"

"Yes. Keeping quiet was getting tricky."

"I wish you hadn't. Oh, I know, you had to because of who he is. Argh. That's why… I don't…"

Festus squeezed her wrist. "Ira, look at me."

She did. His mischievous eyes were solemn. "He loves you more deeply than I've ever seen him love anyone else. Oh, we could use grand eloquent

85

statements and words, but that's the fact of them. You've given him peace where I've given him mischief. You've listened, where I've encouraged. You've helped him face his future; I've helped him avoid it. He wants to love you, see you safe, see your laughter and your soul. He would give you the empire without a second's thought—"

"I don't want the empire! I want to love, to feel protected. All he's done is expose me to gossip and speculation, without a thought for how I feel about it."

Festus chuckled. "Oh, I and Faran have told him that. He stopped inviting you to dance so often because we told him he'd caused you unease. When he asked you to sit at the dais, it wasn't his request but the King's. He finally admitted it to Faran after your talk. He's been tested as much as you have these last few weeks."

"And the meal here with the King? The next thing you'll tell me is that was a test!"

"It was," said Festus lightly. "It was also where your father and the King hammered out the marriage agreement. You took so long to fall to sleep that none of the rest of us slept at all."

"I'm surprised someone didn't spike my drink then."

"We did in the end," admitted Festus with a grin. "Oh, beat me up about it another time. Adeone admired your staying power."

"Did Nia know? Did Faran?" she demanded.

"Nia, no. Faran, yes. He's also Adeone's confidant."

Ira scowled at him. "You've used Nia as a cover in all of this?"

"No." Festus frowned. "I'm furious that's she'll be hurt, actually. Though she should have seen the signs coming last year that Adeone wouldn't ask her. Father tried to dissuade her dreams, but you and Cornelia wouldn't let them die! So before you start blaming myself and Faran for following Adeone's wishes, and the King's for that matter, consider that maybe there's more at fault."

Tears started in Ira's eyes. "I… didn't want her hurt, Fes."

He wrapped her in a hug. "Nor did I. She might not be if you refuse Adeone. He'd accept it."

"But the King has already drawn up a marriage agreement."

Festus hesitated. "It's true, but he likes to be prepared. Adeone wasn't meant to ask you before he left. Think about that. He defied his father to give you time to think. He was meant to ask you at Court."

Ira blanched. "I need to thank him for that, if nothing else."

Festus chuckled. "Yes. You do. Come and sit down and talk calmly."

She sank into her favourite chair and curled her legs under her. She needed time to think. The last revelation had been more illuminating than Festus realised. Adeone was kind and would stand up for himself.

Chapter 13
FRIENDSHIP OR FOLLY

FOUR WEEKS LATER, Ira was as confused as she'd been immediately after Adeone's proposal. If he'd still been in Oedran, it might have helped, but with him on the other side of the empire, the confusion wouldn't die. It wasn't like they had had chance to meet and talk things over. What would be the expectations on her? She decided to write to him. Reading every marriage agreement there was wouldn't tell her what *Adeone* expected. She had to thank him for asking her privately as well and if she was enquiring about expectations, it would appear as though she was considering his proposal seriously.

She tried to work out how soon a return letter would arrive by the mail routes, using her correspondence with her Garth friends as a guide, but the Prince could use special riders at will and those letters would arrive far, far more quickly.

What she hadn't expected was Prince Lachlan calling by the house a week later, asking to speak with her.

"Adeone thought it better that I come, my lady."

"It's very kind of Your Highness."

Lachlan snorted. "Not at all. He wants you to know that there will be Court duties, there will be expectations of fidelity and there is the expectation of children, none of which I can see comes as a surprise to you. There's also a lot of tedious expectations around propriety, but Princess Lilith assures us you know those rules. In private, Adeone assures you that there is only the expectation that you are yourself. He doesn't ask anything more of you than that."

Ira swallowed. "Why are you here?"

"You *are* sharp. Because our mail is rarely private and he doesn't wish you to become the subject of any more speculation. Also, because I'm curious, my lady. I think you still don't know what to do. What is holding you back? Many ladies would have accepted before he could finish proposing."

Ira smiled ruefully. "Your Highness is perceptive. I am an only child, an heiress. There is my family's future to consider. I have no wish to insult Prince Adeone, but this is not a minor consideration. I was brought up knowing the best solution would be a second son. Yet I am facing a future that includes marrying the King's heir."

Lachlan nodded. "I understand the dilemma. It is not one I can help you solve, either. Just know the marriage agreement has made provision for it."

"But not for what happens if I die in childbirth as my mother did," replied Ira carefully.

His searching gaze reminded her that he was the Justiciar, with dominion over the law. He sat as a judge in a court of law. He knew how to read people in ways that went beyond the King's Court.

"Lady Ira, I will speak with His Majesty about that oversight, but the risk is there whomever you marry."

She swallowed. "I know but—"

"The FitzAlcis need to offer more in security than a second son could? I suppose that much is true. Anyone with half your acumen would realise that we are not always the most trustworthy. Whom would you consider your heir if a child did not survive?"

"If there's no distant cousin of my father's then Festus."

"Very well. I shall put that to the King. Is there anything else?"

'Yes,' thought Ira. 'Lex and the fact I love him.' She couldn't say it though. Jilting the Prince for a groom was not something to speak of. Why had the thought she would surfaced? She had to answer Prince Lachlan. "I wouldn't mind knowing about how the household and family duties work, sir."

Lachlan relaxed in his chair. "Oh, I can tell you that, Lady Ira, and a lot I probably shouldn't at the same time." His eyes sparkled. "Would you like to know all Adeone's childhood secrets whilst we're at it?"

She chuckled. "If you'll accept tea and cake by return."

"With pleasure."

As they sat talking, she relaxed. Prince Lachlan could tell a good story and he wasn't as staid as King Altarius. She found herself laughing and joking as though they were closer in age. She understood why Adeone might see him as a nearfather figure.

* * *

The following morning, she was far freer on her ride.

Wynfeld drew level with her. "Are the rumours true? His Highness proposed?"

She bit her lip. "You can't confirm it. I don't know what I'm going to do. It's not exactly an arranged marriage. He fell in love with me—"

"And you with him?" asked Wynfeld.

"I don't know. He's…" She fell silent. 'He's not you,' was what she'd wanted to say. Wynfeld knew her soul already. He would never have to hunt for it or tease it from her with quips and lemons. She entered the woodland, still ruminating.

"Can you help me down?"

He dismounted swiftly and steadied her. They walked for a time, taking little used paths.

"Do you remember the stag?" she asked quietly.

"He brought you good fortune."

"No, he didn't, Lex." She looked at him with clear eyes. "He brought me hope, but life has dashed it. I can be the lady, but what I want to be is here, with your arms around me. I don't fear that future."

He hesitated. "We should stop this, Ira, before it gets us into trouble."

Ira bit her lip. "Do you want to?"

"No," his whisper was so soft the rustles almost hid it.

She found an appropriate branch and hitched her mare to it. Carefully removing the reins from Wynfeld's hands, she hitched his also before putting her hands on his chest.

"What do I do, Lex?"

He started. "Erm…"

"About you, about Adeone, about everything."

He relaxed. "You accept the Prince. There's nothing else you can do, is there?"

"We could elope," she said. "Eventually we could return."

"No. They'd never let you inherit if you refused the Prince to elope with a groom." He chuckled. "I wonder if anyone has ever been that bold with the FitzAlcis."

She laughed softly. "Probably not. I'm not sure I want to marry him."

He picked a leaf out of her hair. "No, but you don't hate him anymore, do you?"

"I guess I don't."

"He's been kind to you. He's been thoughtful. You could do far worse. What would happen if there was a second son who was a good liar, married you for your inheritance and then killed you?"

"That's—"

"Not unheard of. At least with the Prince you've more of a chance of them honouring the agreements drawn up."

She swallowed. "He's not you, Lex."

"No. He's not, but I'm your dream, Ira. I can never be your reality."

She put her head on his chest, listening to his heartbeat quicken. "You feel real to me."

"Ira, please move."

She tightened her grip, looking up at him. His soft eyes caressed her face. Their lips met. She pushed herself closer as his grip tightened.

He broke away. "We should get home, my lady."

"Lex—"

"No. We should get home. This… This can't happen."

She paled. "I thought you felt the same."

"I do, but you're— It can't work! Let's—"

"Pretend it never happened," she finished lamely. She unhitched her mare and turned back down the path. There were too many low branches here for her to mount. When they were on the main path, she refused his help and put her foot in the stirrup. A moment later, she pushed herself up from the leaf litter and cried out in pain. Lex, no *Wynfeld*, felt over her ankle.

"Sprained or badly bruised, my lady. Not broken. Here, let me."

He lifted her up, light as a feather. She rubbed at her face and then cursed. There'd been mud on her hand. Oh well, too late now. They rode home in silence.

* * *

At Macarian House, she let Wynfeld help her dismount and then pick her up to carry her inside. She couldn't put any weight on her ankle. Her father saw them crossing the hallway.

"Wynfeld?"

"Her Ladyship has bruised, possibly sprained her ankle, my lord."

"How? You were riding."

She said, "I wanted to walk for a time, to clear my head, father. It was a stupid mistake."

"I'll send for the doctor. Take her upstairs, please, Wynfeld."

When Wynfeld put her on her bed, she grabbed at his hand. "Don't tell anyone, Lex, please."

"Tell anyone what?" asked Maria, entering.

Their faces gave away too much. Ira knew that by the way her former nurse closed the door on the rest of the house.

"You two are absolute idiots," she raged. She glared at her nephew. "What happened?"

He swallowed. "I can't tell you."

She clipped him around the head. Ira's lips twitched despite herself. There was something so familiar about this scene. She muddied, him getting a roasting.

"Don't give me any of that, young Lex."

Wynfeld sank onto the edge of Ira's bed. She moved her legs instinctively so he could. They exchanged a glance. She pulled a face. Maria would wheedle it out of them now she knew there was something to wheedle.

"We kissed," admitted Wynfeld, blushing. "It wasn't intentional."

"It was on my part," said Ira.

"I thought you'd more sense, Lady Ira. Lex, you go and get cleaned up. I need to sort out this injury. Go on with you."

Once he'd gone, Ira said, "It was my fault, Maria. I've needed his support so much."

"There's a difference between support and that, my lady. Rumour is His Highness has proposed. What were you planning? An elopement?" Maria must have read the truth of it on her face. "Do you really think there's anywhere in the empire that you can hide from the King's agents? There isn't. So either wed Prince Adeone or a lord, but don't think you can marry a groom. Everything you are precludes that option. Now, I've asked for a bath for you and then we'll get that ankle strapped up. You're not going to be riding or walking for quite a time."

* * *

The following day, Nia and Cornelia called by. Ira managed to keep off the subject of Adeone and it was clear that Nia hadn't heard any rumours. Were they just amongst the staff at Macarian House? Or were people keeping them from Nia? She dreaded the day her cousin found out. Did that mean she'd accepted the proposal? If she couldn't marry Lex, was it better to marry the Prince or jilt him? Everyone wanted her to marry Adeone. That much had been clear. She toyed with the threads of her embroidery. Surely there were more interesting things to do when laid up. Cornelia and Nia were chatting away. She wasn't really needed to contribute. For the first time in a long time, she wondered if she ever had been. As she listened, she also heard things she'd never noticed before in the way Nia spoke. There was still childish hope and turns of phrase. Cornelia was far more mature. Was it the age difference? Possibly. She sensed Cornelia watching her and smiled.

"How's your ankle?"

"Ask me something else."

Cornelia chuckled. "Have you heard from Prince Adeone?"

"Why would I have done?" asked Ira evasively.

"I had a letter yesterday. He mentioned he'd written to all of us."

"Oh, I expect it's waiting for me. I was distracted yesterday."

Nia laughed. "You must have been."

Ira twitched. "Well, I did do a bit of damage to myself."

They continued talking for a couple of hours before Nia and Cornelia left. When they'd gone, Ira relaxed. It was silly but she couldn't be herself around them. She had to make a decision but first she had to set things right with Lex.

When Maria brought in her lunch, she asked to see him.

"You can't, my lady."

"I know I shouldn't, Maria—"

"No, you *can't*. He's left."

"What?" exclaimed Ira.

"This morning. He's joined the army. We thought it best."

"No, he can't have gone! I never got to say goodbye."

Maria hesitated. "He said he'd write."

"He never does," mumbled Ira. "It's all my fault."

"Not all. He could have been more sensible. Now, eat your soup."

Ira wiped tears away. "I don't want anything."

"Fine," snapped Maria, unusually sharp. She removed the tray as she left.

Curling into her seat, every emotion Ira had hidden bubbled up. Sobs wracked every part of her body. She'd been reckless and foolish and this was the result. She'd never see him again and her foolishness meant Maria wouldn't see him either, and her old nurse loved him dearly. He'd left so quickly that he must have not wanted to see her. Wanted to escape. Well, that was ironic. It was all she wanted to do. If Adeone hadn't proposed, would she have been so reckless? Probably. Just maybe not so soon.

* * *

That evening, a red dragon messenger appeared asking for a link. She accepted. Prince Adeone appeared at a comfortable speaking distance. He was obviously worried.

"You're hurt?"

"I've sprained my ankle, sir. Nothing more."

"How?"

She explained, telling the same story her father had heard.

"I'll ask Chapa to visit you. No, I don't want to hear your answer yet. I want to know you're well."

"I am, perfectly. Other than a sprained ankle, obviously. Our doctor is very attentive."

Adeone hesitated. "Please."

"Fine. If it puts your mind at rest. How's the review going?"

"Well. I'll be home within a couple of weeks of the Munewid. Oh, my aunt might drop in on you if you can't make Court. I apologise now."

Ira chuckled. "It'll be a pleasure to meet Lady Amara."

"She doesn't faze you? She frightens most courtiers I know."

"Most of those are men, sir."

"True. Oh no. Does this mean I should encourage her not to visit? Will you gang up on me?"

"We may," teased Ira. "It will be a novelty. I shouldn't stop your duties."

"You're kindness itself, Lady Ira."

Chapter 14
ARRIVALS

THE FOLLOWING MORNING, Ira welcomed Doctor Chapa with a wry smile. He matched it.

"His Highness wished me to ensure you won't limp, my lady."

"Is that the reason?" she quipped. "I'm sorry he disturbed you, Doctor Chapa. I'm perfectly well tended."

"Ah. It's what they keep me around for. Now, how did you fall?"

His sharp eyes raked over her face as she told him. "What was your groom doing to let you mount unaided?"

"Obeying my temper," muttered Ira. "It was my own foolishness, Doctor Chapa. Completely and absolutely my fault. Our doctor thinks I need to rest. Is he wrong?"

"Not at all. It seems sensible." He sat down carefully. "This is rather more awkward, my lady, but I am aware of His Highness' proposal. His Majesty has asked me to make sure of your future prospects."

She frowned. "I beg your pardon?"

"That is for children," explained Chapa.

She blushed. "I have my bleeds. I am sure father has told you all that."

"Yes, my lady. He has been most emphatic on the point but I do need to do an examination. Given you're injured, that can explain my visit here. Would you have any objection, therefore, to me utilising the opportunity?"

Hot from head to toe, Ira exclaimed. "I've not even said yes yet!"

Chapa chuckled. "Will you? He's not a bad catch."

She glared. "Are you also part of the conspiracy?"

"No. I'm just His Highness' cousin," replied Chapa. "He's his own worst enemy, in many ways, but he's the kindest heart I know. Oh, he messes around, enjoys his position, but he doesn't like to see people hurt or in pain. He'll make a good husband for someone and an excellent father when it's time. I've never yet known him to intentionally hurt a lady, or, for that matter, a gentleman."

Ira hesitated. It was true. She hadn't heard anyone complain of his actions in that regard. She watched the doctor's face.

"I am still considering what I want to do."

"And agonising over it," replied Chapa with a smile. "That won't help your health, you know. Make a decision, my lady. It's better for everyone."

She sighed. "Do I even have a choice?"

He glanced at the door before whispering, "Everyone has a choice." More loudly he said, "You have to be sure of all consequences, my lady. As do I. May I do the examination?"

Her eyes narrowed. She too glanced at the door. Who was there listening? Her gaze returned to the doctor. He grimaced. Someone was there. She didn't have a choice. If she refused, there'd be consequences.

"Very well."

"Would you like a chaperone, my lady?"

"That would be wise. Ring the bell."

Twelve minutes later, Maria released her hand as the doctor washed his. The examination had been thorough, Ira couldn't dispute that, and she felt oddly ambivalent about it. Chapa was nothing if not professional.

"All in excellent order, my lady," he said with a small smile. "I presume the actual birthing wasn't what caused your mother's death."

Maria said, "It was her heart, Doctor Chapa. The rebellion fever had affected her badly."

Chapa sighed. "It had many consequences." He must have seen Ira's sadness, for he said, "My cousin died birthing Prince Scanlon. Ladies do not have it easy, but I have no concerns for you on that score." He added, "I don't plan to lose anyone else as I lost Eliza."

Ira swallowed. There was something haunted in his voice. "Thank you, Doctor Chapa."

He gave her a slight bow and left.

Maria squeezed her hand. "It's done."

Ira nodded. "Yes, but my decision isn't made."

* * *

Four days before Adeone was due home, Ira attended Court for the first time since her injury. Standing all evening wasn't possible with a sprained ankle, so she had avoided the susurration of gossip that was building around her name. Somehow word of Lachlan's visit and Doctor Chapa's had escaped and the rumourmongers had capitalised on it. Many of them already declaring she'd accepted the Prince's hand. As always, her father accompanied her to her friends before leaving them to talk. Cornelia and Festus welcomed her with smiles, Faran with an amused reserve, Ifor with gallantry and Nia with suspicion laden eyes. None of them asked her outright about the rumours, but there were odd comments such as wondering exactly when the Prince would be back and whether he'd attend Court on his first evening home. Festus fielded most of them and she ignored the others, wishing she could make up her mind.

"Oh, did you hear," said Cornelia, "that Lady Amara's arrived? Lord Ewart and His Majesty are dining together, but apparently Lady Amara might attend Court with Lady Rhian this evening."

Ira shook her head. "We'd better be on our best behaviour then."

Festus snorted. "She'll tell you if you're not. Nia, come and dance."

Once they'd left, Ira relaxed. She didn't miss the fact her friends noticed. "I thought he'd ask me and my ankle still hurts," she lied.

Faran chuckled. "Maybe using it a bit more would help. Will you take a gentle stroll with me, Lady Ira? I promise to hold you up, should you need it. The gardens are especially beautiful at the moment."

Once in those gardens, she said, "I know you know."

He snorted. "So I understand from Festus." He gazed off into the distance. "The King's arranging a marriage for me as well. As soon as my studies are over."

"His Majesty didn't arrange this."

Faran sighed. "No. Apparently, Prince Adeone fell in love with you. It's a good start. At least if you wed him, you'll have met him first."

She hesitated. "That's true, but there'll be no hiding."

"Is there now?" He smiled wryly. "You're the heiress to the Macarian Lordship of Oedran. There's never any hiding for any of us. We have to be seen, we have to become at one with the Court and accept our liege's whims."

"I don't have to swear fealty, Lord Faran."

"No, but your father did and they will expect your son to, unless, of course, he's born FitzAlcis."

Ira bit her lip. "What would you do in my position?"

"Consider whether you have anything to lose by refusing the Prince. Not what you'd stand to gain, that much is clear, but whether you lose anything. Will you lose yourself? Your family? Your friends?" He saw her face. "Nia is not your friend if she begrudges you your chance. She will be upset, she may even be heartbroken for herself, but I doubt she would wish you ill. Festus has been trying to make her look elsewhere for years. As for the rest of us, well, I rather suspect Lord Landis and Lord Rale already have an agreement drawn up for Festus and Cornelia. I'll be returning to Lufian when my studies conclude and I'm of age. I'll likely be married by then as well. The King won't want me choosing my own wife. Too dangerous to have Lords of Provinces deciding their own futures." His lips twitched. "I do rather wonder whom he'll pick for me."

Ira chuckled. "I hope it's someone you can care for."

"His Majesty is an excellent judge of character, so I expect it will be. I have no real qualms over the arrangement. It does mean I can concentrate on other pursuits. Months of angst, years of searching, they're not for me."

Ira watched the gardens. "Can we sit down for two minutes, please, Lord Faran?"

He guided her steps to a bench and steadied her.

"Thank you. I know Prince Adeone is kind; I know he thinks he loves me; I simply can't decide."

Faran nodded. "You've not long left."

"I know." She stared out over the gardens. A lady was walking along the path towards them. Ira pushed herself to her feet and gave a short curtsy, biting back pain. "Lady Rhian."

The King's niece smiled. "I don't believe we've been introduced."

Faran chuckled. "Might I present Lady Ira Macaria, my lady."

"Ah. We won't keep you, Faran."

Rhian took his deserted place and smiled for Ira to resume hers. "There's some interesting family rumours, my lady."

"I bet there are," said Ira without thinking. "I'm sorry, I'm rather—"

"Honest. Let's leave it there. I warn you, mother may pay you a visit."

"I'd be honoured, Your Ladyship. How was your journey from Tradere?"

"Comfortable, but it's nice to be here. I've just visited my sister and baby nephew. I expect I'll soon get questions again about whom I'm marrying and when."

Ira sighed. "It's all anyone ever talks to us about, my lady. As though there isn't another subject whilst we're single."

"You have a point," said Rhian amused. "So, what would you prefer to speak of? How you sprained your ankle?"

"Definitely not. My stupidity is worse than marriage."

"How about Garth then? I've never visited."

"If Your Ladyship would be kind enough to tell me of Tradere."

* * *

Lord Ewart and Lady Amara called by Macarian House the next day. Ostensibly, Lord Ewart had matters to discuss with Lord Macaria.

'I bet he does,' thought Ira. *'My marriage being the main one.'*

She curtsied when Lady Amara was announced. The King's sister might have dropped the title Princess on marriage, but she was still the King's sister and had a greater grasp on the machinations of Court than anyone who lived in another province should have.

"Ah, Lady Ira. It's a pleasure to meet you all grown up. I think our menfolk will be a while."

"Thank you, Lady Amara. Please do sit down. Leo, could we have some tea and cake?"

Once the footman left, Lady Amara eyed Ira. "You can sit down as well, you know. You don't have to wait to be invited to in your own home after we observe the courtesies. Now, tell me who Lex is."

Ira blanched. "What?"

Amara chuckled. "So there is something there. Well, young lady, when you mention someone to Cousin Lilith, she tends to remember and we swap stories in our private letters. Is this Lex holding you back from accepting my nephew?"

Still white, Ira said, "Not at all, my lady."

"And now you're lying. Not a good start. Who is he?"

"I…" She closed her eyes. "The nephew of my old nurse. He worked here until recently."

"Left because something happened between you? Yes. I can see the truth of that. So, be assured I won't tell my nephew, but you need to talk Lex out of your heart. I don't think many know of him, do they?"

"No. We grew up together." Her lips twitched. "He was the brother I never had for so long. We learned together, played together and then I realised we had very different lives to lead. He started working around the house, and I had a governess. We used to manage evenings of games and cards with Maria, my old nurse, but when Lex became a groom, we'd go out riding. Father sent me to Garth to break the bond with childhood, but when I returned, it was like I'd never left, and Lex, we laughed so much. I didn't mean to fall in love with him."

"No, we never do intend to fall in love," said Amara softly. "One day, I'll tell you my story. It caused ructions, so many ructions. It tore my family apart for a time. When did you kiss Lex?"

"How?" Ira sighed. Asking Lady Amara how she knew something was like asking a snake why it had poison in its fangs. "The day I twisted my ankle. He left the day after, without saying goodbye."

"And you're still mourning his departure," stated Lady Amara. "That's difficult, I'll give you that, but he's not coming back."

"I know," whispered Ira. "I wish he'd said goodbye."

A knock at the door heralded Leo with the tray of tea and cake. He set it on the occasional table and asked if Ira wanted him to pour. She shook her head. She wanted him out of the room before Lady Amara said something else.

"What's holding you back from deciding?" enquired Lady Amara once they were alone. "Lachlan says they've sorted out the inheritance question."

Ira bit her lip, passing Amara a cup of tea. "Love. I don't know if I love Prince Adeone."

"Do you know that you don't hate him?"

"Yes, but… It's going to hurt Nia so much as well."

"It'll hurt your cousin because she doesn't know how to listen. There's reasons Adeone could never marry her, reasons we do not speak of, but she should have listened to her father."

"The rest of us didn't help that," admitted Ira sadly. "No-one told me or Cornelia. We're as much to blame."

"Yes, and no." Amara put her cup down. "If you worry about everyone who might resent you, there'll be no end. If you accept Adeone, yes, you'll get a lot of duties and dull monotony with them, but you can help your friends as you can't now. Far be it from me to suggest that you can keep your independence in a way you couldn't if you refuse him. You're surprised by that? Are you independent now or tied to your father's wishes? You're tied to the King's wishes at Court, every presiding lord's wishes, Lachlan's wishes, mine, my daughters' wishes. How many people are you trying to please? You're kind, thoughtful, and generous. You want to help whoever you can. Now imagine whom you'd be answering to if you accept my nephew. The King and him. My brother is easy enough to please, just don't lead a rebellion," Amara chuckled. "Are you surprised to hear it? He is autocratic, yes, but he is not despotic. Father was that and see where that ended: the Bayan Rebellion. Adeone has his mother's kindness and love of life. He's brought his own touch to it, but it's there."

Ira hesitated. "I know he's kind and generous. He's never been anything but a gentleman towards me, but how do I know if I love him?"

"That's not the question to ask in our lives. Can you be his wife? Love develops. Can you sit with him of an evening and listen to his day? Can you soothe a troubled mind? Can you bear his children, your children by him? Can you attend Court, keep your own counsel and smile when your heart is heavy? I think you can."

Ira hesitated. "His touch doesn't awaken me."

"Has he touched you as a lover? Has he touched you at all?"

"He held my hand in the garden."

Amara smiled. "Ira, I can see you as part of our family as I could see Eliza and Ewart. Please know you won't be alone. We're not a large family, but we are an accepting one. You'd gain a brother, aunts and uncles. All of whom are in a position to turn to fractious courtiers and tell them to mind their own business. It has its compensations."

Ira suddenly laughed. "The worst thing about Court is the gossip!"

"Yet we still gossip," said Amara. "Is there more tea?"

When Lady Amara and Lord Ewart had left, Ira sat with her head in her hands, remembering Lex's lips on hers. Festus, Faran, Lady Amara, Prince Lachlan, they'd all given her good advice. She could never have Lex, would likely never see him again. Laughter, scoldings, love all flowed through her mind. She had to decide. She must. Facing Adeone and saying she still didn't know wasn't an option. She wanted to see Lex, not for his embraces, but for his advice. She couldn't ask Festus. Beneath everything else, she'd have put him in an impossible position. Maria wanted her to be happy. Could she be everything that Lady Amara had suggested? If only it were that easy.

Her father entered. "Lord Ewart was very precise and meticulous in outlining His Majesty's expectations. His Highness can't be embarrassed. I have to agree."

Ira swallowed. "His Lordship has taken lessons from Lady Amara."

"Take heed of what it tells you that the FitzAlcis all think the same."

Ira watched him leave. She loved him. He loved her. Where then was the support that was meant to go with love? He wanted her to accept. He needed her to. If she refused the Prince their standing and favour would be nothing for a generation, if not two. Yet, where was his love for her in all this? Others had shown her far more courtesy than he had.

* * *

Ira greeted Adeone the morning after his return with a deep curtsy and a fleeting smile. He watched her for a moment, but addressed her father.

"That's all, Macaria."

She glanced up from her curtsy and saw the smile playing about Adeone's lips as her father bowed and left.

"We'll walk in the gardens, my lady," said Adeone brusquely.

Ira swallowed and pushed herself up. He sounded annoyed. Had Lady Amara broken her word?

He took paths that led them out of sight of the windows. Then, once completely alone, he turned to her. "I'm sorry for what you've gone through since I left for Garth. I'm going to kill my aunt, uncles and cousin!"

Ira chuckled. "They meant well."

There was something in his stance that hadn't been there when they'd last spoken. The glimmerings of position had solidified into something more. His gangling frame no longer appeared youthful.

"How was Garth?"

"As you'd expect." He took her hand. "I need you to know something before you give me your answer. I do not care what my family has said, what pressure they've applied. This has to be your decision and yours alone. I will deal with everyone else. Do you have your answer?"

She closed her eyes. "Yes."

He stilled. "So?"

"Yes, is my answer."

He carefully let her hand drop, staring at her, dumbfounded. "Everyone's been telling me you'd refuse."

She laughed. "Why?"

"Because you hadn't hinted you'd accept! Aluna, protect me. I love you." He pulled her to him, their lips meeting.

She felt his fire. He wanted every part of her, mind and body. His arms secured their hold and he continued as the weight of indecision and anxiety left her. His arms were safe and she let herself fall into his embrace as though there was no past or future, there was only that moment.

CHARACTERS

MACARIAN HOUSE	
Lord Macaria	Lord of Oedran
Lady Ira Macaria	Daughter of Lord Macaria
Maria Wynfeld	Former Nurse
Alexander Wynfeld	Groom
Piers	Steward
Leonard Piers (Leo)	Footman
Jack Pretyman	Head Groom
Abe	Cook
Whyte	Gardener

LANDIS HOUSE	
Lord Landis	Lord of Oedran
Lord Festus	Son of Lord Landis
Lady Feronia (Nia)	Daughter of Lord Landis
William Kadeem	Manservant to Lord Festus

RALE HOUSE	
Lord Rale	Lord of Oedran
Lady Rale	Lady of Oedran
Lady Cornelia	Elder daughter
Finn	Son
Aelia	Younger daughter

RYSON HOUSE	
Lord Ryson	Lord of Oedran
Leila Ryson	Daughter
Elidir Ryson	Son

IRIS HOUSE	
Lord Iris	Lord of Oedran, Advisor to the King
Lord Idris	Son of Lord Iris

AT COURT	
Lord Malachi Faran	Lord of Lufian, Ward of the FitzAlcis
Lord Kenton Parchi	Lord from Anapara
Lord Abbas Atgas	Lord from Anapara
Lord Ifor Daioch	Lord from the Low Plains

IN OEDRAN	
Merchant Netherhind	Cloth Merchant
Master Galdwin	Journeyman
Merchant Latimer	Bookbinder and seller

FITZALCIS	
King Altarius Apolinar	King of the Oedranian Empire
Prince Adeone Altarius	Elder son of King Altarius
Prince Scanlon Amarus	Younger son of King Altarius
Prince Lachlan	Justiciar, King Altarius brother
Lady Amara	King Altarius' sister
Lord Ewart	Lady Amara's husband
Lady Neassa	Lady Amara's elder daughter
Lord Rufus Rathgar	Husband of Lady Neassa
Peaga Rathgar	Son of Lady Neassa
Lady Rhian	Lady Amara's younger daughter
Princess Lilith	King Altarius' cousin
Lord Galwood	Princess Lilith's son
Tyler Galwood	Princess Lilith's grandson
Master Quinn	King's Manservant
Simkins	Manservant to Prince Adeone
Advisor Gillham	Tutor to Prince Adeone
Jenner	A guard

Lexicon

OF THE MOONS

ALUNA	The larger of the two Erinnan moons
ALUNA-MONTH	Four weeks
ALUNAN	The higher section of society
ALUNAN-AGE	Twenty years old. Alunan become adults in law
CISLUNA	The smaller of the two Erinnan moons
CISLUNA-MONTH	Three weeks
CISAN	The lower section of society
CISAN-AGE	Fifteen years old. Cisan become adults in law

ON RELATIONSHIPS

NEAR*	Named when a child is born, *nearparents* act as mentors for a child and would act as guardians should the child be left orphaned. Nearparents' children are *nearcousins*, unless the child lives in the same house, then they're *nearbrothers* or *nearsisters*.
WED-	This prefix denotes relatives married into the family, rather like the suffix *in-law*

OTHER

ALCIA	A guardian of the ancestor's memory
EXARCH	King's Representative and governor of Bayan
MESSENGER	Small magical creatures that can create links between people so they can converse naturally.

Notes on Time

WEEKDAYS		FESTIVALS		
	ALUNADAI		MUNEWID	FIRST DAY OF SUMMER
	CISADAI			FIRST DAY OF THE YEAR
	TRETALDAI		MUNPYRAM	FIRST DAY OF AUTUMN
	IMPERADAI		MUNDIMRI	FIRST DAY OF WINTER
	PENTADAI		MUNLUMEN	FIRST DAY OF SPRING
	HEXADAI		*These festivals are known as Alcis Days*	
	SEPTADAI		*and are marked by both moons being full*	

ON TIME

1 MINUTE	=	60 SECONDS
1 HOUR	=	72 MINUTES (12 X 6 MINUTES)
1 DAY	=	24 HOURS
1 WEEK	=	7 DAYS
COURT CYCLE	=	12 DAYS
1 FORTNIGHT	=	2 WEEKS

Season	Aluna-month	Week	Cisluna-month	Season	Aluna-month	Week	Cisluna-month
SUMMER	CEARAL	1	CEARCIS	WINTER	RALAL	25	RALIS
		2				26	
		3				27	
	TRADAL	4	MIDDIS		ANAPAL	28	NORIS
		5				29	
		6				30	
		7	TRADIS			31	ANAPCIS
		8				32	
	LOWAL	9	LOWIS		BAYAL	33	BAYIS
		10				34	
		11				35	
		12				36	
AUTUMN	MACIAL	13	MACIS	SPRING	TERAL	37	TERIS
		14				38	
		15				39	
	MEITHAL	16	EASIS		GERYAL	40	SOUIS
		17				41	
		18				42	
		19	MEITHIS			43	GERYIS
		20				44	
	SERAL	21	SERIS		LUFIAL	45	LUFIS
		22				46	
		23				47	
		24				48	

POSTSCRIPT

To you, my reader…

Thank you.

I hope you enjoyed *Ties*. This story acts as a prequel to the *Treason and Truth* series as well as a standalone novella.

Please consider leaving a review of this book wherever you feel most comfortable. Reviews really help readers find their next book and help authors find their next reader.

Acknowledgements

Authors rarely get to publication without help and support. They sit and write in snatched hours or minutes. Sometimes stories flow unceasingly from their fingers, clamouring to be heard amongst the din of everyday life. When the last scratch of the pen and click of the keyboard is done, then comes the editing, the interior design, the cover…

My journey has not been solo. From my friends and family who have read, re-read and given me honest feedback to you, the reader that got this far, I say thank you.

This book is dedicated to Sybil Ward who read *Treason* and wanted to know more about Ira. Sybil is the author of the August Grove collection of paranormal mysteries. Her work can be found at sybilward.com

Explore Erinna

Please visit https://erinna.co.uk for more about the Erinnan Legacy or sign up to The Court Newsletter for freebies and news.

BV - #0243 - 190424 - C0 - 203/127/6 - PB - 9781917145008 - Matt Lamination